Short Horror Erotic Stories

love&sex

Cool Erotica

Table of Contents

Short
Horror Erotic
Stories

Story One: Wife's Cousin

Chapter 1

Elva Smith was used to brushing through Twitter and reading novels before going to bed, just like any other day.

However, her distant cousin was going to work along the coast and had a layover in the city for a few days. She temporarily stayed at Elva's house because there were only Elva and her husband, Herman Morgan, living there. Their two-bedroom apartment already had one bedroom occupied by their daughter, so they had no choice but to let her husband sleep on the couch for a few days while Elva and her cousin shared the bedroom.

Elva Smith had a habit of staying up late playing on her phone. Even if she was already extremely tired, she still had to play on her phone for a while before falling asleep. The light from the phone often disturbed the cousin's sleep, causing her to toss and turn all night.

Elva Smith frowned and sighed in her heart. Her cousin was good in every other way – diligent, gentle, and experienced in dealing with things – but she just couldn't sleep well. She would constantly toss and turn in the late hours of the night, which was really annoying.

Elva Smith scrolled through the latest news on Twitter, but her eyes would occasionally glance at her cousin's back. Her cousin continuously turned over every ten minutes, and the old mattress creaked, making it even more noisy.

When the time reached 4:00 in the morning, her cousin finally stopped moving.

Elva Smith let out a sigh of relief and slowly pulled out the knife under her pillow, but then she heard a soft female voice explosion in her ear, "Little Sister, you're not asleep yet?"

Elva Smith turned her head and saw her cousin's head right by her pillow. She froze for a moment, then quickly turned her head back to look at the body that was facing away from her. Her cousin was clearly lying there peacefully, seemingly fast asleep.

Elva Smith thought she was dreaming. The buzzing in her brain grew louder and louder, but the head by her pillow still clung to her in an extremely intimate manner, repeatedly asking that question over and over again.

"Little Sister, you're not asleep yet?"

"Little Sister, you're not asleep yet?"

"Little Sister, you're not asleep yet?"

...

"Little Sister, are you asleep?"

"Oh!!!"

Elva Smith sat up from the sofa, sweating profusely. When she heard the nightmare-like voice, she slapped away the woman's hand in front of her and shouted, "Are you crazy? You keep asking and asking! Are you sick? What's the matter with you?! Why are you pushing me in the middle of the night when I can't sleep?!"

The sharp voice echoed in the not-so-big living room, and the light in the second bedroom was switched on, indicating that someone inside was ready to come out and see what was happening.

Cousin Jessica Lewis lowered her head and stammered, allowing her cousin to curse at her, but what did she actually do wrong? She was just worried that her cousin might not be comfortable sleeping on the sofa and wanted her to go to bed. But this resulted in a round of verbal abuse.

"All this noise! Mom, why are you scolding Aunt again? Can't you sleep in the middle of the night?!"

Elva Smith had her child at a young age, at the age of 19, back in her hometown. She got involved with Herman Morgan, and the two ended up in a small grove, discussing life and harmony, and got caught in the act.

After giving birth to their child, they joined Elva's brother, who was working in the city. Over the years, the two managed to find a way out by specializing in second-hand rental housing. They bought a house and brought their daughter closer to them.

However, due to their daughter not growing up by their side since childhood, the mother-daughter relationship never felt as close as it should be. The slightest displeasure could lead to shouting at her! She really didn't know whose traits her daughter inherited!

"Get lost! All you know is to provoke me with your aunt! Go back to your room and sleep!" Elva Smith, feeling frustrated, pushed the person in front of her and then pushed her daughter, telling her to go back to sleep.

With a 'bang', the door closed, leaving Jessica Lewis alone in the shadows, burying her head and lost in thoughts.

Chapter 2

Soon, Jessica Lewis seemed tired and forgot that the sofa didn't belong to her. She laid down and fell asleep.

Late at night, a sound of the front door opening could be heard as the male host, who had been out socializing, returned. Despite him being drunk, he remained sober-minded.

He was dressed in ordinary black trousers and a blue shirt. His muscular chest stretched out the thin shirt, making it look ill-fitting. With his crew cut hairstyle, he appeared intimidating, but his face could be considered handsome. Standing at nearly six feet tall, he exuded a strong masculine aura that anyone would feel in his presence.

He didn't turn on the lights and quietly went to the bathroom. He intended to take a shower before going to bed. Not turning on the lights was to avoid waking up the other people in the house, his wife and daughter, both with volatile tempers. He was usually easygoing and believed that accommodating his wife and daughter showed his love for them, but it only made their characters more demanding.

Hot water washed away the fatigue from his day. Unable to resist, he soaked in the bathtub for a while, thinking about which client he would take to see houses tomorrow. As he idled away, he absentmindedly played with his large cock.

A thick, semi-erect flesh-colored shaft rested against his thighs. With a few strokes from his fingers, it quickly became rock hard, like a steel cannon pointing forward.

Masturbating himself wasn't particularly amusing to him, so as soon as he got himself ready, he planned to rinse off and go to sleep.

Ever since his wife's cousin arrived, they hadn't had sex for several days. He had a strong sex drive and a large cock. Elva Smith couldn't withstand his assault for more than a few minutes before begging for mercy. Either she used her mouth or her breasts to bring him to orgasm.

Although Elva Smith's hole wasn't tight, her large breasts were quite satisfactory, which pleased him.

At the thought of his wife's big, white breasts, Herman Morgan's inner desires started to burn. The image of his cock being squeezed between her breasts and occasionally sliding out from the cleavage lingered in his mind, refusing to dissipate. His recently relieved cock quickly became erect again, straining against his pants.

He annoyedly clenched his teeth and threw the towel on his head onto the armrest of the sofa, not even bothering to check if there were any obstacles on the sofa. He sat down without noticing, and immediately heard a sharp cry of pain. Realizing something was wrong, he quickly stood up and looked backward.

The living room was pitch dark, with no hint of light. However, in such close proximity, he could still make out the figure of a woman sitting halfway on the sofa. It was Jessica Lewis, his wife's cousin. Her hair was disheveled, her eyebrows slightly furrowed, and her delicate face displayed a trace of hidden pain.

His gaze shifted to her thigh, which she was touching. In the darkness, her fair and slender legs almost brushed against his eyes. The legs seemed a bit red, indicating that he accidentally sat on her thigh when he sat down earlier.

Out of reflex, he muttered, "Sorry, I didn't know you were here."

Then furrowing his brow, he asked, "Why are you sleeping here? Didn't you go back to your room?"

Jessica Lewis hesitated as she looked at him, but ultimately didn't say anything. She just bit her lip and gently massaged her own thigh, lost in her own thoughts.

Herman Morgan's entire family had explosive tempers and had never encountered this kind of timid and hesitant behavior before. He felt a bit impatient, but when he saw the red mark on her thigh, his anger subsided.

He sat back down and, for some reason, reached out to touch her softly, saying, "Let me massage it for you."

Chapter 3

The man's voice was deep and powerful, but his actions were somewhat rough, indicating that he hadn't done this before.

With calloused hands, his palm burning hot, he placed it on Jessica Lewis' smooth thigh, creating a sharp contrast with her fair leg, which had a touch of sensuality.

After massaging for a while, Jessica Lewis noticed that the man's posture seemed a bit off. She secretly observed and discovered the reason, but she didn't say anything. Instead, she suddenly straightened her leg. Without any precautions, Herman Morgan's hand slipped down along the smooth skin, getting stuck between Jessica Lewis' thigh and her panties. He even touched a few pubic hairs that were visible from the edge of her underwear.

He was taken aback, wondering if this woman did it on purpose or it was an accident. Then he lightly tugged at the corner of his lips and pretended it was an "accident," slipping his hand into her underwear.

"Sorry, cousin-in-law. It's too slippery, I wasn't paying attention," the man explained, feigning concern. But his hand didn't show any remorse as he continued to explore deeper. He found a slippery area and reached a conclusion in his mind, becoming even more audacious.

"It's... it's okay, brother-in-law. It's too dark, without light, it's easy to touch the wrong place..." Jessica Lewis softly responded, not knowing if she was comforting him or herself.

The man sneered inwardly. She was already soaking wet, yet trying to make excuses. But he didn't expose her. Instead, he calmly adjusted to a more comfortable position, lightly caressing and teasing her folds with his fingers, occasionally sliding his fingertips along the crevice, leveraging the moisture present.

"It's too dark indeed, but it's too late to turn on the lights and wake them up. Cousin-in-law, please be considerate," he said, his voice filled with cold amusement.

Jessica Lewis felt that while the two of them were speaking earnestly, their actions in stimulating each other were becoming too intense. But she couldn't bear to get up. She whispered and gasped, her legs unconsciously tightening.

"My brother-in-law's fingers are so thick... I'm sure his work is very hard... oh... very tiring..."

Herman Morgan had already inserted two fingers into her pussy at this point. He couldn't help but want to curse, as this slut was too wet and tight, making it difficult for him to move his fingers.

Suppressing the impulse to immediately pull out his cock and fuck her, he thought to himself that if he didn't give her a good experience with his big cock, it would be hard to have a next time. Even if he did, he didn't know if there would be a next time. What if she turned out to be useless like his wife? That would be disappointing.

With this in mind, he became more patient and gradually added a third finger as the woman's pussy gradually adapted to the intrusion.

Jessica Lewis held onto Herman Morgan's wrist, her pussy being fucked by his fingers. But she was still unsatisfied. She forcefully spread apart her tender flesh with his fingers, allowing her clit to directly touch the skin on his wrist. She shamelessly started grinding back and forth.

Herman Morgan was dumbfounded. He had never seen such a slutty woman before. Feeling the wetness on his wrist and the sensation of the woman's tender flesh against his own skin, his cock was about to explode.

He held back again, trying to resist, but he couldn't hold back any longer. He suddenly withdrew his hand, lifted the woman up, leaned her back against the sofa, and spread her legs open, positioning himself on top of her.

He had put on loose beach pants after taking a shower. These pants couldn't function as underwear at certain times, such as now, as his rock-hard cock was remarkably large and long. Due to the angle, it had already poked out of the pant leg, even lifting it up. Seeing this situation, Jessica Lewis didn't need any insertion. Her arousal was already flowing out in bursts, making her both tingly and thirsty.

Chapter 4

She gazed at Herman Morgan tenderly and reached over to put her hand in between them, grasping his huge cock firmly. With a strong tug, she pulled down his beach pants, hanging them on his thigh.

Herman Morgan raised an eyebrow, looking somewhat suggestive, but Jessica Lewis paid no attention to that. She held his balls in her hands as well and couldn't resist licking the big head of his cock. Slowly, she tasted the entire length of his big cock, savoring it like an ice cream.

The freshly showered cock had a hint of the scent from the shower gel. Jessica Lewis licked and sucked all over, not missing a drop of the fluid from his balls and the gland at the tip.

Herman Morgan enjoyed the sensations of the woman's lips and tongue while stroking her long hair. He thought, does this woman have a big cock fetish? He heard that people with this symptom have a strong desire for big dicks and want to be fucked by them every day. If he guessed correctly, then maybe there would be days when he could have his way with her. One thing was for sure, his own cock had the right assets.

Jessica Lewis held onto his cock for quite some time, reluctantly returning to the position of leaning back against the sofa with her legs open. It seemed as though she was afraid the man wouldn't understand, so she actively used both hands to hold up one leg, completely exposing her lower body in front of him, as if saying, "Fuck me quickly."

Naturally, the man wouldn't hold back. He looked at this slutty woman and felt a bit regretful. If he had known that she was so wet and wild, they wouldn't have wasted a few days. But it wasn't too late. He set a small goal for himself—to let her sleep with his semen inside her every day, starting from tonight!

The rock-hard shaft didn't even need any support. The woman's ample lubrication was already prepared to welcome its arrival. The man thrust forcefully, and due to the vigorous impact, their flesh collided with a smacking sound, startling the two of them in the silent night of their stolen pleasure.

At this moment, neither of them cared if they would wake up the sleeping persons. The man's cock was just too big, and Jessica Lewis's pussy was too tight. Although they had already done some foreplay to prepare, the intense fucking made it hard for them to endure.

Herman Morgan slightly pulled back, just that one movement almost made him break a sweat. Her pussy was wet and tight, like a real little mouth sucking his cock relentlessly, her soft flesh squeezing his glans and causing him to let out a slight gasp involuntarily.

Damn, it feels so good!

After pausing for a few seconds, he believed that enough rest time had passed for the woman to adapt to his size, so he began to move.

Herman Morgan held onto Jessica Lewis's waist and thrust himself into her again and again, going deep and shallow, hitting the deepest spot with each thrust. It was so intense that Jessica Lewis almost screamed, but luckily she managed to react in time and covered her mouth with her hand.

Herman Morgan looked somewhat dissatisfied with the woman's action. Her crying while having her mouth covered and her eyes closed, it looked too much like rape. So he used more force in fucking her pussy and used his hand to pull away the hand covering her mouth.

"Why cover your mouth? I'm not raping you. What's with the pained expression on your face?"

Jessica Lewis opened her eyes, her teary gaze softened, and her voice became softer.

"Brother-in-law, your cock is just too big. It fucks me so good that I almost pass out. If I don't cover my mouth, what if I scream? My little sister is still inside... Oh... It feels so good, being filled up like this. I want to keep sucking my brother-in-law's cock..."

Herman Morgan's eyebrows relaxed a bit, but when he thought about his wife and child sleeping in the next room while he was fucking her cousin...

Fucking hell! It made it even more pleasurable!

Damn! How can this woman be so good at fucking?!

Chapter 5

Herman Morgan felt hotter and more satisfied as he fucked, even having a feeling of all those years being wasted. As he continued fucking, he also felt a hint of familiarity, as if he had freely indulged himself on someone's body like this before.

He swung his cock, gripping the woman's big breasts with his hands, his expression gradually becoming wild. He didn't notice that the woman he was fucking had gradually become motionless, nor did he notice her pale skin starting to turn blue. All he felt was that his big cock had entered a place that could bring him immense pleasure and ecstasy.

That place seemed to have a life of its own, transforming into countless mouths that simultaneously massaged his cock, squeezing and thrusting, making him feel incredibly pleasurable.

In a place he couldn't see, beneath the woman, maggots were continuously surging out of her pussy. Some were crushed into a pulp by his cock, but most of them were like flies finding rotten meat, crazily attaching themselves to it. Countless maggots wrapped around Herman Morgan's proud cock, but in his eyes, it was Jessica Lewis voluntarily tightening her tender pussy, diligently serving him.

Jessica Lewis looked horrifying at this moment, her face purplish, covered with strange spots, devoid of any signs of life.

The maggots flowing out from her body didn't seem to cause her any sensation. She just stared at the man on her with a strange look, her eyes only showing the whites, stiff and unblinking. As the man's movements became more frenzied, the changes in her body became more evident. Anyone seeing her wouldn't think she was a living person.

When she saw the man eventually being ejaculated by the maggots, spraying all over the sofa, she curved her mouth upwards, raising her stiff arm to wrap around the man's neck.

"Brother-in-law, let's continue tomorrow. It's too late today, if I don't go back to the room and my little sister wakes up and sees I'm not there, she'll suspect something."

The man failed to notice anything wrong. Satisfied from earlier, he casually waved his hand, already categorizing this woman as his possession, thinking there's plenty of time ahead. He had had a good time today, so it was time to let her go back to her room and sleep.

The man went to the bathroom with a foul smell and bugs all over him, but Jessica Lewis turned back to the bedroom.

Jessica Lewis didn't turn on the lights, just silently lay down. The old mattress made a long creaking sound under the pressure. She turned over, facing her younger cousin who was frowning impatiently, clearly having been disturbed by the noise from the mattress.

Jessica Lewis leaned closer, her voice gentle, like whispers between lovers. She opened her mouth and asked, "Little Sister, you're still not asleep? Sister is feeling cold, so maybe let Brother-in-law warm me up with his big cock. I believe you wouldn't mind, right? After all, back then, because I was scared of the cold, you had Thomas, that scoundrel in our village warm my body before. That time wasn't very warm, but this time it should be better. Thank you, younger sister, you're so...considerate..."

The nineteen-year-old girl, naive yet malicious, blinded by jealousy at seeing her older cousin dating the most handsome young man in the village, had lured her cousin out on a winter night and let a scoundrel rape and kill her. And now she was seducing that handsome young man, who had taken her sister's place as the victim, with a fragile demeanor, and it seemed she finally got what she wanted...

How could this be allowed?

Herman Morgan's cock, in life it belonged to me, and even in death, it will only be mine...

"Sorry to disturb you, but my house will be under renovation for a while, and it might inconvenience you and Elva Smith for some time... I will pay the rent!"

The woman felt shy and embarrassed, feeling that she was causing too much trouble for her rarely seen cousin.

"It's alright, cousin. Just settle in and stay at the bedroom with Elva Smith. I sometimes come back very late at night, so you don't have to worry about me."

...

"Why have I never heard you mention having a cousin before?"

"She's a distant relative, and I almost forgot about her. We used to play together as kids, I think? It wouldn't be right to not help when she's in the same city... Oh well, we're family, so it's fine for her to stay for a few days."

Well then, my dear cousin, please excuse the inconvenience...

Story Two: Perfect Boyfriend

Chapter 6

"Karen Pink! Are you even listening? Every time I talk to you, it's like it goes in one ear and out the other!"

"I've told you, I'm searching, searching, searching! It's not that easy, you know? You can't just find a job immediately when you say you're looking!"

Here we go again, it's always like this! Constantly being pressured to find a job, but it's not easy to find one now. She has no experience and no education, am I supposed to settle for any random job?

Ever since Karen Pink graduated, her parents have been pushing her to find a job. Normally, a fresh graduate should have no trouble finding a job.

Speaking of this, Karen Pink feels a hint of regret deep inside. If only she had studied hard, why did she spend her days reading novels and playing games? In the end, she graduated from a low-ranking vocational college.

She throws herself onto the couch, staring blankly at the ceiling, imagining what could have been if she had studied hard before. She pictures herself holding a prestigious university diploma, gradually climbing the corporate ladder like in those workplace novels, and finally finding a boyfriend who is even better than herself and getting married.

Her thoughts gradually immerse her in this fantasy, and when she comes back to reality, she realizes that time has slipped away silently. She had been daydreaming for three or four hours!

But she doesn't really mind, she doesn't have a job now and spends all day at home. Even if she wastes some time, it doesn't really matter, right?

She thought this way, but deep down, a sense of panic began to rise.

All her friends had found jobs, and she was the only one still at home. Although she constantly made excuses for herself, she couldn't deny the reality.

She knew that this couldn't go on. She clasped her chest, suddenly feeling breathless. After a while, she thought maybe it was just her imagination, or perhaps it was just the stress from job hunting lately. She just needed to take a break.

She quickly finished her lunch and returned to her room, lying down. She knew it wasn't right, but she couldn't stop thinking, "It's okay, just take a rest. I need to rest to have the energy to search for a job."

She hypnotized herself like this and gradually fell asleep.

"Director Pink, here are your documents."

An indescribable voice sounded in her ear, and Karen Pink looked up in confusion at the source of the voice.

"Hmm, this person looks familiar," she thought subconsciously, but her hand reflexively accepted the documents.

She looked around and saw a neat and elegant office with a desk filled with various papers and a computer. She was sitting in front of the computer, and next to it was a potted plant, perhaps to absorb radiation from the computer or to alleviate office fatigue. And in front of her was the person who called her Director.

Oh, yes, she was the director of this company. She was young and successful, and she must have a handsome boyfriend, right?

As soon as the thought came to her, her phone on the desk rang, displaying "Boyfriend" on the screen.

Karen Pink answered the call in confusion, but realized that her phone seemed to be malfunctioning as she couldn't connect. She became anxious and started sweating, feeling as if something bad would happen if she didn't answer the call. She desperately tapped on the screen.

Chapter 7

When she woke up, the ringing of her phone reminded her that it had indeed rung, but it wasn't the nonexistent boyfriend from her dream, it was her best friend.

Taking a moment to calm down from the anxious feeling in her dream, she slowly answered the call.

Her friend invited her to go out and play over the weekend, but considering her recent situation and her wallet, she declined the invitation.

After she hung up the phone, she fell asleep unknowingly. Strangely enough, the dream from earlier continued!

The call with her boyfriend didn't end, and the name displayed on the screen changed from "Boyfriend" to a person's name, Regan Ford.

Dreams are illogical, and Karen Pink was the same. She just somehow knew that this person's name was her boyfriend, who had called her earlier.

This time she finally answered the call, and the voice on the other end was particularly pleasing to the ear, but it also sounded like it was at a distance, creating a sense of unreality.

She furrowed her brow, wanting the person to speak up, but reminding herself that he was her boyfriend, she tried to be patient instead of rushing the conversation.

She listened for a while until she heard the other person seemed to be inviting her to dinner in the evening. She immediately agreed, and images of a luxurious restaurant and a romantic scene with roses being held by a handsome and gentle man came to mind. She couldn't help but feel excited.

By the time she finished work, Karen Pink grabbed her bag and walked out of the office. The bustling company entrance was no longer filled with traffic; instead, it was covered in a foggy mist with a white, hazy sky enveloping the building behind her. She became disoriented and suddenly forgot where she was supposed to go. What did Regan Ford tell her earlier?

When Karen Pink woke up, it was already dark outside. She checked the time and was surprised to see that it was already midnight.

Since she had not closed the window, the curtains would occasionally be blown by the night wind. She felt a headache coming on and realized she was a bit hungry. Once again, she had missed dinner and couldn't recall if she had even eaten lunch before.

Perhaps she did eat, otherwise she wouldn't just be slightly hungry, but rather very famished.

She thought to herself that skipping a meal wouldn't make much of a difference. After a while, she stopped pondering these questions and decided to check the refrigerator for something to eat.

She got up, closed the window, and turned on the lights. Looking at the empty fridge, she realized belatedly that because she hadn't gone grocery shopping in a long time, she had been relying on takeout for meals, and the refrigerator had long been empty. That's when she went to the kitchen in her slippers and found some noodles to fill her stomach.

She felt drowsy and her mind was more muddled than before. No wonder old people often say that sleeping too much isn't good. But thinking about sleep... she yawned, feeling like she was getting sleepy again.

It was already nighttime, and she probably should go to bed! Without much struggle, she returned to her bed.

She remembered that Regan Ford said he would come to pick her up by car, so it suddenly dawned on her. She waited at the company entrance, and her colleagues leaving work beside her looked at her with envy, saying, "Waiting for your boyfriend again? Your relationship is so good!"

Karen Pink smiled reservedly, trying not to show too much sweetness. She remembered that she was their superior and shouldn't be too close to her subordinates. So she nodded and said, "Yes, he insists on picking me up from work every day, no matter what I say. By the way, it looks like it's going to rain soon. You should go home too, be careful not to get caught in the rain later."

In the next moment after she finished speaking, the sky grew even darker. Suddenly, a raindrop fell on the employee's head. Surprised, they looked up and apologetically smiled at Karen Pink, saying, "Well, Director Pink, I'll be heading off now. See you tomorrow."

Chapter 8

On the deserted street, Karen Pink stood alone, watching as a white hearse slowly appeared around the corner. She smiled happily, as if she could already see her boyfriend's gentle face.

The car stopped in front of her, and a man wearing a white suit and exuding a handsome aura stepped out. In his hands, he held a bouquet of vibrant roses, his eyes filled with stardust as if the woman before him was his entire world.

His voice was tender and clear, no longer distant like through a microphone.

"Did you wait long? There was a bit of traffic on the way. My little princess, aren't you angry, right?"

Karen Pink gave him a playful glance, her voice sweet, "Why would I be angry with you?"

She secretly appraised him. Was this her boyfriend? He was truly tall and handsome! Such a high-quality man, and she managed to win him over! It was truly... amazing!

Unaware of what she was thinking, the man simply extended his hand, a slight smirk on his lips. "So, may I have the honor of inviting my little princess to dinner?"

He playfully winked, igniting a fiery sensation in Karen Pink's heart. Blushing, she nodded and placed her hand on his arm.

The car seemed to have been driving for a long time, yet it also felt like just a moment. They arrived at the entrance of the restaurant, exactly as she had imagined. The interior was lavishly decorated, with a serene ambiance. Each table was properly spaced, providing a comfortable distance between guests.

Regan Ford led Karen Pink to their seats, by the window where they could see pedestrians on the street. However, it seemed like the glass had good soundproofing, as she couldn't hear any noisy sounds.

"Darling, what would you like to eat? Order whatever you want. I hope we can have a perfect night..."

The man's words seemed to have a hidden meaning. Karen Pink blushed and simply buried her head in the menu.

As she looked through it, she froze. Was she mistaken? There was nothing on the menu pages. She flipped a few more pages, only to find that it was completely blank, just a white piece of paper. She suddenly became lost in thought, her mind drifting...

After what felt like a while, she heard the sound of cutlery. Snapping back to reality, she saw herself holding a knife and fork, cutting into the steak on her plate. The man across from her was eating his meal as if nothing was out of the ordinary.

"What's wrong, baby? Not feeling hungry? The food in this place is pretty good. Didn't you always want to try it?"

Regan Ford seemed to notice Karen Pink's absent-mindedness and asked with concern.

Karen Pink paused for a moment upon hearing his words. To conceal her distracted state, she quickly forced a smile and explained, "Nothing. It's probably just exhaustion from work. The taste of the food here is indeed delicious."

After speaking, she put the sliced steak into her mouth. Suddenly, she felt like she was being torn apart. Her taste buds told her that the steak had no taste, akin to chewing on wax. But her brain told her that the steak was extraordinarily delicious, tender and juicy, making her taste buds want to explode.

She stopped chewing, staring blankly at the man elegantly enjoying his meal in front of her.

Karen Pink woke up with a splitting headache, accompanied by hunger. She didn't know what time it was or how many meals she had missed. All she felt was extreme hunger and a pounding headache.

The dream was so vivid that she could recall the intricate patterns on the steak. She swallowed saliva and forced herself to get out of bed, intending to grab her phone to order takeout.

Her phone was plugged in on the computer desk, just a few steps away from her bed. But she realized that her legs were no longer capable of supporting her to complete the simple task of getting her phone.

As she tried to stand up and took a step forward, she fell onto the hard tile floor. Pain overwhelmed her brain. She tried to use her elbow to support herself and crawl back up, but she was horrified to find herself utterly powerless. She mustered all her strength to flip over and lie on her back on the ground, gasping for air...

She wondered if she was dying. Why was reality so cruel while dreams were so beautiful? She closed her eyes and reminisced about everything she experienced in the dream. Her brain gradually became muddled, and she sank back into the embrace of sleep...

Chapter 9

The steak in her mouth was delicious, and the violin played by the staff on the stage was enchanting. Karen Pink was also satisfied with the admiring glances from passersby outside the transparent glass.

Suddenly, she felt a warm hand caress her leg, slowly moving upwards. She tightened her grip on the cutlery, and her heart raced...

This, this is happening in public, so thrilling?

She discreetly glanced at the man beside her. She didn't know when he had sat down next to her. She couldn't see his actions due to the tablecloth, but she could feel his strong and slender fingers reaching under her skirt. He lightly touched her panties and gently stroked her clit, sometimes using his palm to cup her entire outer genital area, squeezing and kneading it along with her underwear.

His actions contradicted his gentle demeanor and can be described as quite wild, with a hint of roughness, but not enough to hurt her.

Instead, due to the continuous stimulation of her external and internal genitalia, a wave of pleasure surged through her body. She used her hands to hold onto the edge of the table, trying to resist this unfamiliar sensation as much as possible, but to no avail.

The man looked at her tenderly, observing her struggle. He directly moved the table away.

The surrounding diners were surprised by the commotion and glanced over, but once they saw what was happening, they lost interest and turned their heads away.

Regan Ford squatted beneath Karen Pink, removing her panties. He then lifted her skirt, lightly parting his thin lips as he gently sucked on Karen Pink's clit, teasing and sucking it slowly.

"Oh... No... Regan... It's too stimulating. We should go home. Oh... Oh... Be gentle..."

Karen Pink's body arched back, providing Regan Ford easy access to play with her pussy.

While teasing her tender clit, he didn't forget to undo Karen Pink's clothes, revealing her plump and milky white breasts.

With her clothes in disarray and the lower hem lifted, exposing her plump and moist pussy, only revealing her two large breasts, the diners around them calmly continued eating in this grand and magnificent restaurant.

Observing this debauched scene, Regan Ford's eyes showed appreciation.

As if he had had enough of her clit, he started using his tongue to lick between her folds. Every time his tongue slid vertically, the large folds would visibly open and then close again. Struggling back and forth a few times, a flowing stream gradually emerged.

He collected some with his tongue, smearing it all over the woman's nipples, and once they were covered in the lustful fluid, he took a mouthful and savored the taste.

Karen Pink never imagined that one day she would have her breasts sucked in public. Her bright red nipples were faintly visible in the man's mouth, with saliva dripping down the milky white breasts, creating a watery trail.

His hands were not idle either. One finger gently pulled and teased one side of her large folds, drawing circles and occasionally sticking to the tender flesh before parting. Occasionally, he would generously touch the dripping entrance of her pussy with his finger, but never entered. How could Karen Pink endure such intense teasing?

She caressed Regan Ford's spine, her voice filled with a pleading tone, "Heron, fuck me, please. Put your big cock inside me. I can't take it anymore... My pussy is so itchy, so empty... I want you to fuck me..."

The man lifted his head, seeing Karen Pink's eager and unsatisfied expression, he lightly chuckled, "Don't be impatient. I will definitely satisfy you today..."

He leisurely undid his pants, and a completely mismatched and ferocious cock sprang out.

Chapter 10

His cock had a perfect shape but was enormous in size. Veins covered its surface, and the color was rather dark. The two heavy testicles were piled beneath the rod due to the pants, making the whole package appear even more ferocious.

He lightly tapped his smooth glans with his fingertips and said softly to Karen Pink, "Give me a good licking, and then I'll play with you."

With his elegant and handsome appearance, dressed in a pristine suit, he undoubtedly looked otherworldly. Yet, he uttered such vulgar words. Karen Pink felt a tingling sensation in her heart and involuntarily crouched down, following his request.

As soon as his cock entered her mouth, Karen Pink tasted a hint of fishy smell. She licked it with the tip of her tongue; it seemed to be coming from the urethra. She thought that if she licked it clean, the fishy odor would disappear. So, she spat out the cock and used her lips to suck the tip, using her tongue to tease it. When she felt she had sucked enough, she took the cock back into her mouth.

Regan Ford didn't say a word, allowing her to curiously explore and play with his cock.

Karen Pink had seen a few erotic movies and imitated the way the actresses use their mouths to pleasure a cock. However, this cock was too large. So, she recalled how the women in the films sucked cocks.

She held the cock with her hand, using her tongue to massage it gently. Then, she used her lips to suck on each patch of the cock, while her hand delicately fondled the two testicles.

The more she sucked, the more she found it delicious, and the emptier she felt between her legs. Regan Ford's gaze grew intense, not because of anything else, but because he noticed a long strand of lascivious fluid dripping from the woman's raised white buttocks, almost touching the ground.

With a raised eyebrow, he suddenly supported his cock and unexpectedly shoved it into the woman's mouth, thrusting back and forth without waiting for her to adjust.

The woman's mouth was forcefully penetrated by the cock, causing her eyes to roll back due to its size. However, the man showed no sympathy. Instead, after forcefully thrusting deep, as the woman's throat constricted, he released a hefty load of thick white semen directly into her throat.

"Cough... cough..."

Karen Pink covered her mouth and started coughing violently, with a lot of semen choking her airway and making her extremely uncomfortable.

But when she thought about how this was her lover's semen, how her lover had ejaculated in her mouth, a hint of sweetness rose in her heart.

Regan Ford still had that gentle look on his face, despite his cock being exposed, covered in semen, and having just been forcibly inserted into his girlfriend's mouth. But anyone who saw his expression would be deceived by his face, thinking he was a gentleman.

Using the hand covered in the woman's arousal, he gently caressed Karen Pink's face, gazing at her with affection.

"Alright, alright. Look at how my baby endured it. Honey, I'll give you my cock now."

After saying that, he lifted the woman up and had her straddle his arm. After a slight adjustment, he slowly inserted his large cock into Karen Pink's pussy.

As the cock went in, the strand of lascivious fluid hanging from her opening finally snapped and fell onto the clean ground.

Regan Ford carried Karen Pink while still penetrating her and walked to the floor-to-ceiling window. He gently put her down and flipped her over, positioning her with her butt against the glass, raised high.

After only two thrusts, he pulled his cock out. Karen Pink, who had just taken a taste, felt extremely unsatisfied deep inside.

She didn't have any objections to this position. She just tried her best to lift her butt higher, wanting the man to penetrate her sooner and make it more comfortable.

Regan Ford didn't disappoint her. Seeing her slutty butt raised high, he slapped her voluptuous cheeks with both hands and spread them apart, thrusting his cock inside.

The pleasure from below became too intense. Karen Pink's hands started to sweat, and she felt as if she couldn't hold herself up against the glass any longer.

She moved her palm upwards, enduring the man's relentless onslaught from behind. Her pussy was stretched to the limit by the large flesh rod, the collision between their lower bodies, the friction between the flesh rod and her walls, and the stimulation hitting her sensitive spots with every thrust. Karen Pink felt like she had experienced a death.

Every passerby on the street was drawn to the sight of them fucking. Some showed no interest and continued on their way, while others stopped and watched.

Those who stopped were usually men, with faces of various kinds, but the same protruding cocks and lustful gaze, as if they wished to push away the man fucking her and replace him with their own cocks.

Some even shamelessly took off their pants and started stroking their thick cocks with their own hands. Whenever this happened, the man behind her would increase the strength and speed of his thrusts, as if he too felt jealous.

She also saw a few women, perhaps finding her expression too pleasurable, curious about how big the handsome man fucking her actually was. They crouched down and looked up through the glass, trying to get a closer look at where their genitals connected.

While watching, they would reach into their own panties and touch themselves. At this moment, Karen Pink would intentionally tighten her pussy, causing the man to moan in pleasure and the women outside the window to turn green with envy.

After being surrounded by countless onlookers, the man finally let out a slight breath. After roughly fucking Karen Pink a dozen times, he ejaculated deep inside her.

This dinner can be said to be exceptionally satisfying and lengthy. When it was time to pay, there were hardly any people left in the restaurant.

In the car, the two exchanged a lingering kiss. Taking advantage of Karen Pink's distraction, the man slipped a ring onto her ring finger. Karen Pink swore that this was absolutely the most beautiful diamond ring she had ever seen.

The man gently kissed her face and asked, "Darling, will you marry me? Let me take care of you for the rest of our lives. Will you be with me forever?"

One week's later, after Karen Pink's mother returned from her trip, she tried to contact Karen Pink for a week but couldn't reach her. Finally, she used her spare key to visit Karen Pink and discovered that her daughter had passed away with a smile on her face.

It was unclear what had happened to her. The house was in a mess, with the refrigerator filled with rotten food. Her body had become emaciated, lying on the floor with sunken cheeks. Her entire body seemed drained of blood, yet there were no visible wounds. Surprisingly, there was a satisfied smile on her face. Her lifeless eyes were fixated on a poster of the sexy male star Regan Ford hanging on the wall, a gentle and handsome man with a mysterious smile on his face.

As if a gentle and passionate voice were asking,

"Will you be with me forever?"

"Yes..."

Story Three: Marry A Ghost

Chapter 11

"Oh, your daughter is 28 years old, right? When is she going to bring her boyfriend over to meet us?"

The summer sun was still shining brightly, even though it was already six or seven in the evening. The hot summer air was steaming, accompanied by the occasional buzzing of mosquitoes, which added to the irritation.

A few women had finished dinner early and sat outside on small stools to enjoy the coolness. One woman, wearing a floral print dress, fanned herself with a handheld fan, speaking in a loud voice that made the chubby aunt sitting next to her shift slightly.

The woman speaking paid no attention to the annoyance of others and continued to flirtatiously interact with one of them.

The woman being asked appeared to be in her forties, with many noticeable sunspots on her cheeks. Nevertheless, she was the most striking among the women present, and her figure hadn't lost its shape. She also held a fan in her hand. Among the group, she wasn't considered young or old.

Hearing the woman's words, she paused the slow movement of her fan for a moment, then gently raised the corners of her eyebrows and chuckled. She seemed very friendly and said, "Yes, she's 28 now. But there's no rush for this. When it comes to marriage, young people should choose someone they like. When the right time comes, if Violet brings her boyfriend home, I will definitely let you all meet him."

The chubby aunt who had shifted her position leaned forward and chimed in, "Yes, that's right! I heard that people in the city don't marry early! Take her time and choose well. When she marries someone from the city, she'll become a city person too!"

Another person pushed her lightly and scoffed, "Can you please watch what you say? Can't Violet become a city person on her own terms? What nonsense..."

Violet's mother couldn't help but smile and cry at the conversation. She quickly changed the subject to defuse the situation, "Alright, alright. Let's not worry about that. By the way, I heard that Frank's family just became grandparents a few days ago. Isn't the baby adorable?"

The attention of the group instantly shifted, and they engaged in lively chatter about the new grandchild in Frank's family.

The person they were just talking about, Violet, full name Violet Adams, comes from a hard-working rural family. Since she was young, she has listened to the villagers talk about how successful college students are. She had the aspiration to go to college but unfortunately, she was not able to achieve it and only managed to study at a vocational college.

However, she had a lively personality and was considerate towards her parents. The family had a great relationship. At her age, there were not many unmarried girls in the village, but her mother always comforted her, saying there's no rush and that good people will come along. On the other hand, her parents in her hometown endured the disdainful looks of the villagers.

She knew that the people in the village didn't have much entertainment. After a hard day's work, they relied on gossip to relax. They even knew things about certain families that their own members may not be aware of. The people in the same village were already spreading rumors and helping to spread them.

She knew that her parents would be mocked and ridiculed at home because of her situation. This made her anxious and eager to find a boyfriend.

She knew this was not right. They were living in modern times, and educated people shouldn't be affected by gossip and societal judgment. However, in life, very few people could truly ignore rumors and gossip.

She privately asked her non-single girlfriends to introduce suitable men to her. Her friends were very helpful and had introduced several men to her. She seriously considered each one, but perhaps due to bad luck, each one had issues that she couldn't accept to some extent.

Chapter 12

For example, there was a blind date who was extremely stingy, to the point where Violet Adams forgot to bring tissues and asked him for one. He handed her a tissue, the kind that you can buy at the supermarket for two dollars a pack, and then asked her for two dollars...

And then there was another one who seemed fine at first, but after chatting for two days, he wanted to book a hotel room with her. He had an ordinary yet confident demeanor, and everything he said implied, "You'll make a fortune by being in a relationship with me. Hold on tight to a man as exceptional as me." Violet Adams almost vomited in his face.

And then there's the backup guy from her friend who introduced potential partners to her...

Too many stories like this, and over time, Violet Adams became somewhat disheartened. Blind dates are unreliable; maybe she should rely on fate instead!

In reality, there was someone she had a good feeling about, but unfortunately, he didn't even know her.

The neighborhood where she lived was a bit far from the city center, and she wasted a lot of time commuting every day. However, the security of the neighborhood was decent, and the rent was cheap, perhaps because it was remote.

That man also lived in the same neighborhood. She noticed that he lived in the adjacent building, but she didn't know on which floor.

She didn't need to pay particular attention because their commuting routes overlapped. They probably had similar work schedules since they would leave their respective buildings at the same time every morning.

She estimated his height to be over 1.8 meters, carrying a trendy casual bag, looking fresh and not like a typical office worker, more like a college student. And that face, it absolutely fit the adjective that's popular on the internet now... um... what was it called? Oh yeah... "First love face"!

Every time Violet Adams followed behind him, her heart would race. She really wanted to go up and strike up a conversation, saying anything would be fine, like, "What a coincidence, I see you every day! Our work schedules seem similar!" Just some meaningless but natural conversation topics. But she was timid.

She always felt that men with handsome appearance could not possibly not have a girlfriend. At the very least, even if they didn't have a girlfriend, they must be popular with the opposite sex. She, on the other hand, has an average appearance, no charismatic personality, and she was not outstanding. She hardly has any shining qualities, so there's no way someone like him would be interested in her. Maybe he would even dislike this person who randomly approached him. Every time she thinks about these things, she recoils.

Today, however, something strange happened. The weather was gloomy, looking like it was going to rain. She just walked out of the building and realized that she forgot to bring an umbrella. After hesitation, she decided to run back and grab one.

Sure enough, even until she left the neighborhood, she didn't see that familiar figure. She felt a little disappointed, but the thought of seeing him later in the evening made her happy again.

But when she came home in the evening, she still didn't see him. She thought maybe it was just an accident, that she missed him because she took time to get the umbrella. However, she didn't see him for several days afterwards.

Violet Adams started to panic. She wondered if he had moved? But recently, she hadn't seen any moving company people coming and going!

This is how modern society is. They say it's easy to stay connected, but if you don't have the other person's contact information, it's actually quite simple for someone to disappear from your life, and others have no way of finding them.

Violet Adams is that "others."

Chapter 13

A week had passed, and Violet Adams had already gotten used to not subconsciously looking for that familiar figure on her way to and from work. She believed the person must have moved away, and after feeling down for two days, she let go of those emotions.

It's normal to come and go, after all, they had no relationship whatsoever. She began consciously developing the habit of checking the news on her phone while walking in the morning. This way, she could shift her attention and stay updated on current events, killing two birds with one stone. She was quite satisfied with it.

Saturday morning had fewer people, as many had weekends off and didn't have to go to work. But she, with her single day off, was still on her way to work.

As she approached the last traffic light before the subway station, something inexplicably moved her and her gaze shifted away from her phone. It was then she realized that she had stepped on something under her feet.

She instinctively looked around, seeing a couple of pedestrians, perhaps like her, who had to work on a Saturday. But everyone was mostly focused on their phones, not paying attention to others.

She redirected her gaze and bent down to pick up what she had stepped on.

It was an object wrapped in red paper, looking bulging. She had no idea what it could be, and she hadn't even felt it under her foot! She must've been absent-minded...

After briefly contemplating, she unwrapped the red paper, thinking that if it was money, she would hand it over to the police to find the owner.

But inside, it wasn't money. Underneath the red paper was a layer of red cloth, and hidden beneath that was the contents.

Inside were a pair of gold earrings, a pair of gold rings, and a gold necklace. Below them were two pairs of silver bracelets, and underneath all that was a photo.

She picked up the photo and looked at it, only to find that she recognized the person in it! The person in the photo was the handsome young man she yearned for every day!

It seemed like a passport photo, and she held it in her hand, looking at it over and over again, realizing that the person she had been daydreaming about was truly amazing-looking, even in a passport photo!

The man in the photo had a particularly bright smile, but it seemed that the photo had been kept for a long time, as there were traces of dampness and subsequent drying on the back. It didn't look like it had been well-preserved.

Now Violet Adams was in a bit of a dilemma. That man had already moved away, so how could she return the items to him?

Subconsciously ruling out the option of handing it over to the police, she was secretly pleased. Wasn't this a ready-made opportunity for her to establish a connection with him? Returning the items, wouldn't he be grateful to her? Maybe even treat her to a meal or something? With one thing leading to another, wouldn't it naturally progress?

The problem was that she couldn't find him right now. She didn't even know his name. So she decided to wrap up the items again and put them back in her bag, preparing to plan this matter slowly, for now, she needed to go to work.

With a yawn, Violet Adams shut down her computer and glanced at the time subconsciously... It was already one o'clock in the morning... it was so late...

She stretched lazily, and for a moment, it seemed like she could hear the crackling sound of her bones.

Working overtime every day, can this company ever get better? And the overtime pay was only so little, it was more of a token gesture... Some companies don't even provide overtime pay, they say...

While thinking about work, Violet Adams didn't waste any time and swiftly checked the windows, turned off the lights and locked the door, heading towards the elevator.

The office building they were in had at least dozens of companies, so the corridors were quite long. But the bright lights gave her a sense of security. Even though Violet Adams considered herself an atheist, darkness itself had a tendency to amplify people's inner fears, and it had nothing to do with ghosts or spirits.

Fortunately, the elevator happened to be on her floor, so she didn't have to wait, which improved her mood a bit. She walked briskly to the elevator, pressed the button, and got in. However, when the elevator reached the fourth floor, she heard a 'ding' sound, and the elevator stopped.

Violet Adams was curious, but considering it was so late, it was probably someone else working overtime, just like her!

The elevator doors opened slowly, and a tall and slim young man walked in, holding a few envelopes in his hand and a backpack slung over his shoulder. He seemed to be chewing gum. Violet Adams felt a bit dizzy.

Chapter 14

A refreshing scent with a hint of sweetness filled the elevator, emanating from the young man. With every breath, she could smell his scent. Violet Adams's heart raced, as if she needed to hold onto the elevator wall to steady herself.

Yes, this young man was the handsome guy she thought had moved away. She felt a bit nervous and thought she should say something at this moment, anything would do! After all, she had found his belongings, right?

But her voice seemed to get stuck in her throat. This habit of being unable to speak when nervous made Violet Adams feel like crying out of frustration.

Trying to control her emotions, she was about to speak when unexpectedly, the young man turned around and gave her a friendly smile.

"What a coincidence! I see you again. It seems like we can meet every day!"

She had heard him speaking on the phone when she passed by him before. It was that kind of pleasant, youthful voice, smooth and slightly gentle, filled with vitality.

This is clearly my line... Violet Adams thought with surprise, but her mouth quickly responded, "Yeah! I was going to say the same thing. It seems like we can meet every day! But I haven't seen you these past few days, it seems."

For some reason, Violet Adams felt the young man's gaze deepen, and he smiled as he explained, "I went back to my hometown for a while. My parents are getting older, and their health hasn't been great, but luckily it was a false alarm." Then he curiously asked, "Why are you leaving work so late? Isn't your company upstairs?"

Being looked down upon by someone she liked made Violet Adams, who was only 1.6 meters tall, feel a bit embarrassed. It always made her feel a bit inferior when someone she liked looked at her so seriously.

She moved her foot but ended up standing still, just without looking at him anymore. She turned her gaze toward the elevator doors and complained in a seemingly relaxed manner, "Yeah, our company is on the eighth floor. We've been working late a lot recently, and now I'm the last one left, lonely, going home..."

The young man nodded, thought for a moment, and said, "I'm also working overtime, actually. I came to get some documents. But if we're being precise, you're not alone in working late. You have to include me as well. I'll keep you company!"

As soon as the words fell, the elevator suddenly fell silent, and the atmosphere became unexpectedly ambiguous. Both of them stopped talking, one realizing that their words could be easily misunderstood, and the other purely surprised and stunned by the seemingly teasing remark.

In this silence, the two of them walked out of the elevator. Violet Adams only then realized that she had absent-mindedly followed the young man to the basement parking garage. She awkwardly glanced at the man beside her, unsure if she could salvage the situation by going back now...

However, the young man lightly chuckled and patted her head, saying, "Why don't you ride with me today? After all, we live in the same neighborhood, so it's convenient."

What could Violet Adams say... To be able to ride in the car of her idol and spend more time together, of course she nodded and agreed!

Once they were in the car, the young man spoke again, "Actually, from now on, we can go together. It seems like our morning and evening schedules are pretty similar. I start work at 8:30, and you probably do too, right? By the way, I've said so much but haven't asked for your name yet! I'm Mike Thomas, what's your name?"

Violet Adams cautiously glanced at him from the passenger seat before answering, "I'm Violet Adams. Our work schedules align, but wouldn't it be too much trouble for you every day? How about I pay for the gas?"

Chapter 15

Naturally, Mike Thomas didn't accept her offer to pay for gas. In the end, they agreed to meet at the entrance of their building at 8:00 a.m. every day, and Violet Adams would ride with Mike Thomas to work. If the timing allowed, they would also walk back together after work. They exchanged WhatsApp and phone numbers for easy communication.

Mike Thomas' WhatsApp avatar, like himself, had a simple and minimalist style. It was a simple handwritten word 'Mike', but Violet Adams couldn't get enough of looking at it. It felt as if staring at it for long enough, she could see through the words and get a glimpse of how he wrote that word.

She could imagine his every pose and expression, as if it was a treasure just installed on her phone. She was eager to learn everything about him, and she started to feel like she was turning into a fanatical fangirl.

Even when she arrived home, she felt like she was still in a dream! Her mind was filled with every little detail of their time together, and the more she thought about it, the sweeter it felt.

He not only didn't move away, but today they even spoke to each other and he even patted her head while they rode in his car! They even made plans to commute together every day in the future!

Wow!

It seems like working overtime isn't always a bad thing. She gently rubbed her cheeks and laughed happily.

The next day, with an anticipation-filled heart, she indeed saw Mike Thomas waiting downstairs. He didn't have a backpack today, instead he greeted Violet Adams while holding a laptop, giving him a hint of an elite demeanor.

Well, she admitted that maybe beauty is in the eye of the beholder; even if he held a pancake in his hand, she would still find him incredibly classy...

For the next month, they commuted together to work every day. Her colleagues in the company noticed her radiant smile every day and teasingly asked if she was no longer single, as if she had been soaked in the bliss of love...

In reality, that was far from the truth! She bit her lip, realizing that she still only had one-sided feelings for him. However, she believed that he might have some favorable feelings towards her as well, maybe even more than just a little... Because recently, they seemed to be getting closer and closer. Their conversations no longer felt awkward, and they occasionally touched each other, like patting her head, pinching her cheeks, or lightly tapping their heads together.

Moreover, besides crossing paths during their commute, they frequently chatted on WeChat and would go for late-night snacks together. However, it seemed like they had eaten too much because every time the shop owner would look at her with strange eyes, which made her feel extremely embarrassed. After twice of encountering this, they decided to order takeout instead and eat together. The meeting point was in Violet Adams' living room, so she diligently cleaned the house every day, afraid that her idol would find her home messy.

Months passed like this, as if it were a normal day. They had just finished dinner at Violet Adams' house and were lying on the sofa, trying to digest. Maybe the atmosphere was too good, but Violet Adams felt that Mike Thomas's gaze towards her was particularly tender.

Just as she was about to ask him what was going on, he suddenly locked eyes with her and said, "Violet, will you be my girlfriend?"

Caught off guard, she was frozen for a moment by this confession.

This... Although she had dreamed about it before, but she didn't mishear, did she? Was Mike Thomas asking her to be in a relationship with him?

Perhaps she was just too happy and dumbfounded. Besides the joy and surprise in her mind, there was also a big question mark - why?

But maybe love is just unreasonable like that. She quickly pushed aside her doubts and didn't let untimely self-doubt affect her happy mood.

She couldn't possibly reject such a good thing, so as soon as she reacted, she immediately accepted.

Chapter 16

Violet Adams didn't know how things had turned out this way. It seemed that certain things naturally fell into place after they became a couple, like, for example, having sex.

It was normal for couples to engage in such activities, and since they truly liked each other, Violet Adams didn't have any reservations about premarital sex. Although she was actually a virgin, Mike Thomas said he was a virgin too, so it seemed even more appropriate.

The premise was that Violet Adams wouldn't be fucked until she cried...

On the two-meter-wide bed, the highly elastic mattress had always been the source of Violet Adams' sweet dreams. The pink bedsheet she carefully selected was pleasing to the eye, but at this moment, it was in disarray due to the two careless individuals on the bed.

Violet Adams lay naked on the bed, while the man behind her also had his body exposed. However, he appeared to be studying a serious subject, with a troubled expression replacing his usual light-heartedness. He spoke to the woman with a slightly whiny tone, "Baby, I've tried, but it seems a bit difficult, I can't get in, can you help me?"

Violet Adams' face turned completely red, with tears still lingering in her eyes from the pain she had just experienced. She turned her face aside, indicating a hint of avoidance, and pressed the bedsheets against her cheek. She mumbled, "I... I don't know either... I thought in those movies, you just aim and it goes in... It must be because your cock is too big!" Her tone became more confident as she uttered the final sentence.

It must be because his cock was too big that it hurt her! So, the two of them ended up getting up halfway and searching for "educational materials" to study on the spot.

Mike Thomas appeared stylish and trendy, but in reality, he was a programmer by profession and had always been a good, obedient child who followed his family's instructions. Although he had seen his fair share of movies, he had never actually put what he saw into practice. As for Violet Adams, she hadn't been in a relationship for 28 years before meeting Mike Thomas!

After watching two erotic movies together under the covers, they both felt ready again! They concluded that it was mostly because they hadn't had enough foreplay! Let's try again!

This time, it seemed to be right. Mike Thomas followed the instructions in the video and began playing with Violet Adams' perky breasts.

Men seemed to have a natural talent for this kind of thing. He stared at the small nipple for a few seconds with a focused gaze, then cupped the full breasts and kissed them.

His agile tongue circled around the nipple, gently tugging and pulling it with his lips. Then, he extended his long tongue to engulf a large portion of the milky skin, sucking on it voraciously. The whole breast was covered in his saliva, which added an erotic touch. He didn't neglect one breast after finishing the other. With both hands gripping the base of each breast, he playfully shook them, as if he had found a fascinating toy, unwilling to let go.

Violet Adams couldn't take it anymore. Being fondled by a man's large hand for the first time, not only was she thoroughly kissed, but also being treated in such a provocative manner. Her heart felt full, as if something was about to overflow. She weakly clung to Mike Thomas' back, futilely trying to press him closer to her chest.

Mike Thomas, for some reason, followed the force of Violet Adams and buried himself within her ample bosom. He had noticed earlier that these breasts were at least a D-cup. This idea of being nestled between breasts was something he had secretly fantasized about during adolescence, and unexpectedly, it was being realized today.

After greedily suckling a few mouthfuls of the breast's fragrance, the soft and pliant bosom was irresistible to him. He couldn't help but lick and drink from it. However, once he remembered that there were even more delicious places to explore, he sensibly prepared to leave it for now.

Violet Adams was so aroused by the 'learning' session with Mike Thomas that her juices were flowing. His perfectly face pressed against her own breast, he seemed to be enjoying every second, occasionally turning his head to alternate between sucking on the seductively red nipples. This was a scene she had never even dared to imagine before. Her heart tingled with excitement, and a pool of desire fluid gushed out of her entrance.

After playing for a while, he released the mistreated breasts. From the gentle kisses on the chest, Mike Thomas moved to Violet Adams' waist, where there was some soft flesh. This was the consequence of not exercising and indulging in late-night snacks. However, Mike Thomas didn't seem to mind this bit of extra meat at all. On the contrary, he touched and kissed it over and over again.

"Mike Thomas... I'm already wet down there... Look at me..." Violet Adams wanted to gently urge him to penetrate her. She consciously bent her legs, hoping that Mike Thomas would also caress her pussy.

The young man spread her legs apart and used two fingers to touch her pussy. His fingers were covered in her wetness, and he suddenly said, "Violet, call me honey, and here..." He kneaded her pussy and continued, "Didn't we watch a video together earlier? What did they say? How should you say? Hmm?"

Violet Adams blushed, stuttering in her reply, "S-slit... Honey... Violet's pussy is soaked. Please fuck me with your big cock..."

Mike Thomas smiled in satisfaction, and with the lubricated fingers, he inserted them into her tight entrance. As his fingers went in, they squeezed out some more juices. He regretfully watched them fall onto the bedsheets, but his finger movements did not stop.

He twisted and thrust his fingers back and forth. Every time his fingers grazed her tender flesh, it sent shivers down her spine. Violet

Adams finally felt the pleasure of being penetrated and couldn't help but urge him on, "Oh... It feels so good. Honey, your fingers are so skillful... I want it faster...more... Oh..."

Hearing the woman's plea, the young man added another finger, trying to stretch her entrance further. He then continued to gently thrust his fingers. Tears welled up in Violet Adams' eyes, her brows furrowed, and continuous moans escaped her lips. She suddenly tightened her grip on the bedsheet beneath her, her lower body trembling. It seemed like she was about to climax.

However, at that moment, the man stopped. Violet Adams opened her eyes in confusion but before she could say anything, her voice was muffled, "Hmm... No... Not yet... It's still too big..."

Taking advantage of the impending climax, the man boldly thrust his big cock into her pussy. Her already soaked pussy, softened by his fingers, was not difficult to penetrate. Yet, Violet Adams still felt a sensation as if she was being split open.

She moved her legs and tried to contract her walls when the cock stopped inside her. As she felt herself fully stretched, she heard the man grunt, "Violet, don't squeeze, it's too tight... squeezing hurts..."

She sheepishly stopped her probing and softly suggested, "Honey, your cock is too big... It's already fully stuffed in. We can't move, so why don't we just rub against each other like this?"

Since she hadn't experienced the pleasure of being penetrated before, Violet Adams hesitated, but there was no way Mike Thomas would allow her to escape at this moment.

He couldn't help but laugh, with his cock still inside her. How dare she say such things? Today, he must fuck this woman senseless so that she craves him every day!

Chapter 17

Violet Adams' legs were held in Mike Thomas' arms, and she could feel the muscles on his arms that touched her skin, as well as the man's hot temperature, which almost melted her.

Her lower body was slowly penetrated by the man, with each shallow and deep thrust making her feel like he was about to pull out, only to be slammed back in the next moment. What's even more frightening is that Violet Adams, accustomed to this rhythm, would automatically tighten her walls when the man was pulling out, as if wanting to keep him inside.

She gradually began to feel a hint of pleasure inside her tunnel. With the back-and-forth friction of the cock, this pleasure accumulated. When the man accidentally hit a certain spot, her whole body trembled, a strange sensation rushed to her scalp, and a large amount of fluid gushed out from her pussy.

Mike Thomas, noticing the difference, had a slight change of mind. Then, like entering a new world, he increased the pace of his thrusts, passionately pounding against that spot while holding onto Violet Adams's big butt.

The sounds of splashing water and the smacking of their buttocks merged into a captivating symphony, arousing both of them even more.

Unable to resist, she grabbed her own breasts and vigorously massaged them. Since she hadn't been fucked enough, her moans were still somewhat shy. Even when she reached the most pleasurable point, she could only let out futile "mm, oh" sounds, without much dirty talk.

But Mike Thomas wasn't satisfied. He was thinking that he had to teach Violet to express herself more during their releases, so that their lovemaking would be even freer and more comfortable.

While considering how to train this woman to better suit his desires, he continued to thrust his cock into her pussy, splashing their legs and buttocks with the copious amount of arousal dripping from her.

Although it was indeed pleasurable, she couldn't withstand this intense storm as a novice in such matters. The excessive pleasure accumulated in her body, making her feel like she was about to explode—both satisfied and uncomfortable.

As the man's body moved on top of her, he teased her ear, sensually licking the sensitive spot behind it. Occasionally, he would ask in a hoarse and seductive voice if she liked it, if she wanted him to be rougher, if she wanted him to fuck her from behind, or if she wanted him to penetrate her back hole and cum inside her every day before she went to work...

She was about to go crazy. She was gripped by a man and he forcefully inserted into her sensitive spots. The man also used words to tempt her. Suddenly, she whimpered, leaned over and kissed his face, and begged softly, "Mike Thomas... Mike, my dear, please...oh...I can't take it anymore, please give it to me...is that okay? Oh... too much...so comfortable... I can't handle it..."

Mike Thomas paused, as if he was stimulated. He held Violet Adams tightly and thrust fiercely. This time, there were no restraints, only wild and intense movements, filling the entire passage. After the final deep thrust, his cock pressed against her cervix and released hot semen. Violet Adams could feel the throbbing of his cock, and after he finished ejaculating, he ground inside her a few more times, as if trying to squeeze out the remaining semen in his testicles, before finally pulling out.

There was a scent in the air that could only be found after a sex. Mike Thomas stroked Violet Adams' back with one hand, as if comforting her and caressing her.

He lay on his side, with his long and thick cock still covered in the fluids of both of their bodies. His other hand held his cock and moved it up and down, occasionally leaning down to kiss the woman who was still immersed in the afterglow of orgasm. He looked lazy and satisfied.

After a while, Violet Adams regained focus and saw this scene.

What does it feel like to watch a handsome guy pleasure himself lazily? The answer is arousal!

Some remaining semen oozed out from the meaty, flesh-colored shaft, hanging on the glans, where white semen mixed with the red tip made Violet Adams's mouth dry. The man's hand didn't stop, still stroking up and down. He asked Violet Adams while stroking, "Do you like what you see? Is my cock pleasuring you, Violet?"

As he asked this question, the hand that was caressing Violet Adams' back had moved to her breasts and began playing with them.

Violet Adams had just experienced an orgasm, but he aroused her again. Blushing, she replied, "It looks... looks good... your cock is making me feel so good... it's pleasurable..."

The moans escaped Violet Adams' lips as she was being fucked in her pussy.

Mike Thomas kissed her nipple gently before pressing his lips against hers. Their tongues entwined passionately, and he whispered, "My adorable Violet... I want to fuck you every day. Shall I fuck you relentlessly, turning you into a hungry little slut who can't get enough of my big cock?"

Violet Adams had her mouth and tongue explored, while her breasts were still in the man's hand. She couldn't help but wrap her arms around his neck, completely immersed in the passionate kiss. She felt fulfilled and overflowing with emotions.

But the fleeting moment of tenderness lasted only a few seconds. The man, still kissing her, guided her hand to hold his cock. The intention was clear.

Violet Adams felt her palm burn for a moment, but then relaxed and firmly gripped the precious member in her hand. Who would have thought that a few months ago she could only quietly watch his back and now she was able to hold his cock in her hand?

Pride surged within Violet Adams as she pushed the man onto the bed. They shifted into a 69 position, with Violet on top, her ass facing the man lying down, and her mouth in front of his large cock.

She stared at the weighty shaft and, following what she had seen in videos, stuck her tongue out to lick the glans. She licked the frenulum, cleaning the drops of cum that lingered on it. Then she opened her mouth wide and tried to take the cock in, struggling as her mouth stretched to its limits. She was about to spit it out when suddenly her whole body trembled.

She felt something wet, slippery, and warm pressing against her pussy. She knew what it was. It was the man's tongue, giving her oral pleasure, licking the pussy he had just fucked.

Every sensation seemed to converge on that point beneath her, and the unexpected pleasure made her head tilt back. The big cock slipped out of her mouth with a loud smack, hitting her face.

But she didn't care about that anymore. She felt the man's lips wrap around her dripping pussy. Then his agile tongue pushed apart her folds, teasing her entrance a few times before forcefully plunging it into her wet hole. Overwhelmed by the sucking and licking sensations, Violet Adams felt her legs go weak. She eagerly took the neglected cock back into her mouth, working it with her tongue, while a thought that seemed out of place arose in her mind...

Just now, she was completely filled with his semen, right? His cum hasn't been scooped out of her little pussy yet! When Mike Thomas licks her, he will definitely taste his own cum...

Oh... Why is it that when she thinks about it, her whole body heats up...

She couldn't help but imagine the scene beneath her right now: Mike Thomas's tongue penetrating, mixing with her cum, while she is licking his cock...

Chapter 18

As Violet Adams suspected, Mike Thomas held her plump, raised buttocks with both hands, as if he had seen it in some strange scientific illustration claiming that women with this kind of butt shape produce more fluids. And indeed, it was true.

When Mike Thomas was being pleasured by her licking his glans, he noticed the thin streams of lustful liquid about to drip from her slightly parted folds. He smelled the aromatic scent, a sweet and juicy mixture with a hint of promiscuity, and with no regard for whether he would taste his own cum, he went ahead and licked her buttocks.

The taste was as sweet and fragrant as he had imagined—sweet, juicy, and laced with a hint of lasciviousness. He couldn't care less and casually licked her delicate folds before thrusting his tongue into her wet hole, pushing it past the opening like a hungry mouth, causing even more fluids to gush out along the walls of her pussy, which he eagerly received into his mouth. He curved his tongue, teasing the thin entrance, and indeed, he heard the woman's unbearable moans...

Violet Adams held the throbbing cock in her hands, heated by her licking. Her pussy was overflowing with arousal from the man's tongue, and she wasn't satisfied with just using her mouth to experience it. She wanted to ride it, to take this big thing inside her already moist hole.

Her face flushed, she was on all fours, her ass raised high, and the man's assault on her pussy showed no signs of slowing down. Finally, when he pulled his tongue out and licked her back hole, she felt her body release the accumulated pleasure. What she didn't know was that, unintentionally, she had squirted for the first time, leaving the man confused and covered in the surging lustful liquid.

He held her and sat up, the juices dripping from his cheeks. He wiped his face and only then realized what had just happened—she had squirted, the legendary gushing orgasm!

He felt a little happy, and he placed the soft woman in bed, assuming a doggy style position. It seemed like he wanted another round. He still felt sorry inside because it was a waste to finish on her face, but unfortunately, she moved her mouth away in that second!

The young man was full of strength and energy, but Violet Adams was somewhat afraid. The terrifying pleasure just now had exceeded her limit. She felt like she was going to be ruined and naturally didn't want to be sprayed again. So she quickly reached out to protect her private part and scolded, "No more! If you do it again, I'll really be licked to death on the bed! Honey...... I don't want it anymore, okay?" Her tone softened towards the end, hoping to dissuade the other person with a bit of coquetry.

Mike Thomas thought for a moment and decided to let her off for now. But he still touched Violet Adams' raised private part and laughed, "Alright, if you don't want me to lick, then let it go. Are you really sure you don't want me to penetrate again? Look at your tight little hole, it's clearly so thirsty."

As he spoke, he lightly patted her private part with his large palm, creating a splash of water.

Violet Adams pursed her lips and opened her legs a little wider before turning back, saying, "Honey, put it in. Fill my hole with your big cock and shoot it into my womb..."

Mike Thomas naturally fulfilled her wish, pressing his erect cock down a bit and thrusting into her entrance.

The wet and tight tender flesh instantly closed in, squeezing this big cock from all sides. Both of them let out satisfied sighs.

Being penetrated by the cock once again, Violet Adams felt an unprecedented satisfaction. After two rounds of intercourse, her private part had already become very soft from being played with. She didn't feel any pain when the cock entered, only a fulfilling fullness and a pleasurable friction. After pausing for a moment to ensure that the woman could fully accept his cock, Mike Thomas held her buttocks and started fucking her, each thrust vigorously distorting her rear.

Being slapped on her buttocks forcefully like a fierce storm, Violet Adams had a feeling as if a huge object was inserted into her cervix, and she felt a fearful sensation of being torn apart inside.

Fear and pleasure mingled in her brain. This orgasm came fast and intense, and before he had even thrust a few times, she screamed and tightened her inner walls, making the man frown in discomfort. This time, the man didn't deliberately seek her sensitive spots, but with his large cock, he could hit them from any angle. Combined with the fact that the doggy style position easily leads to orgasm, after a hundred deep thrusts, the woman's hot liquid sprayed onto his glans, causing a slight shiver. Mike Thomas relaxed, and his thick semen shot into her hole once again.

Violet Adams was completely exhausted, and in the end, Mike Thomas carried her to take a shower. The intense sexual activity had made a mess of the bed, with their fluids and stains covering the sheets. Since they didn't have time to change the sheets, they made do with sleeping in the guest room for the night.

A good night's sleep was interrupted by the sound of a ringing telephone that woke Violet Adams up.

The peculiar melody sounded somewhat eerie, but due to her exhaustion, she had no energy to move. She felt lazy and hazy, and in this state, she felt like she had forgotten something. But her clouded brain didn't give her much time for thinking.

Fortunately, it was a day off today... she thought, squinting her eyes, feeling like she was about to fall back asleep.

In a daze, she heard a woman's voice with a thin and gentle yet strange tone singing softly in her ears along with the melody:

The moon shines bright, heart in a flurry,

The bridegroom takes a new bride in a hurry,

Rosy lips, fair face, a scholar he is,

Blush on the cheeks, a bride who's his.

If love should last for all eternity,

Turn back and gaze forever, we'll be.

The voice was sharp, the melody stretched out, and the ending note seemed to have a hook. Accompanied by the eerie ringtone, Violet Adams suddenly felt like a bucket of cold water had been poured over her. She instantly woke up and realized that it was Mike Thomas' phone, which he had left under the pillow, ringing.

It seemed like Mike Thomas was also awakened by the ringing, and the melancholic female voice continued singing. Just as she repeated the line "If love should last for all eternity," the owner of the phone managed to answer the call. The haunting ringtone disappeared, and Mike Thomas, upon hearing the voice from the phone, seemed to glance at Violet Adams for a second, but it might have been her imagination. He didn't look at her.

He exclaimed "Mom..." into the phone, then sat up and mouthed the words "Sorry, I have to take this call" to Violet Adams, before walking towards the living room. He seemed reluctant for his own phone conversation to disturb her.

Violet Adams instinctively smiled at the man, then relaxed and burrowed back under the covers.

She covered her head with the blanket but couldn't fall asleep no matter how hard she tried.

The unsettling ringtone kept looping in her mind. It should have been such a beautiful morning, but it gave her goosebumps instead.

She quietly complained about the man's taste in ringtones, then suddenly felt sweet inside as she couldn't help but wonder what Mike Thomas and his mother would talk about on the phone. Would they mention that he had a girlfriend? His mother would surely inquire about his girlfriend's job and family background, right?

She felt a bit frustrated. It seemed like she hadn't really talked to Mike Thomas about her own family situation. Of course, he hadn't talked much about his either. They were just like infatuated students, not considering so many things, and simply acting on their intense desire for each other.

Chapter 19

Violet Adams didn't know when she fell asleep. As she was lost in her thoughts, she drifted off into a dream and woke up again, already in the afternoon.

She didn't check the time, but she knew it was already noon...

She was awakened by licking. Mike Thomas slipped under the covers and, while she was still deep in sleep, shamelessly used his tongue to lick and tease her most intimate parts. This time, it wasn't as hurried as the first time; he took care of every detail. She woke up while he was kissing and licking her clit.

The stimulation was intense, and when she woke up, she couldn't help but moan softly. That was when she noticed the man nestled between her legs.

Seeing Violet Adams wake up, Mike Thomas promptly uncovered the blanket and threw it aside. His mouth was covered in a mixture of her juices, but his face wore a familiar smile.

"Are you awake, my sweet Violet?" he asked.

It was as if he greeted her at the door every morning with a bag on his back, instead of just raising his head from between her thighs moments ago.

Looking at her ideal man in this state, Violet Adams felt that she would gladly let him fuck her to oblivion!

Perhaps it was really the allure of lust, but before she even had a chance to eat, she had a taste of his cock.

As Mike Thomas stroked her mouth playfully and kissed her lips, he whispered, "Baby, are you hungry? Shall we have some cock before we eat?"

Who could resist this temptation!!

As Violet Adams took his cock into her mouth and started to lick and tease, she only then realized that they had started again. But the man's lips and tongue were so skilled and nimble that they quickly drew her into a whirlpool of desire, leaving no room for any other thoughts.

When it was all over this time, Violet Adams was really starving. But there was cooked rice in the rice cooker and some takeout dishes on the table. She just needed to heat up the dishes in the microwave to eat.

After they were full and satisfied, they lay on the couch. Violet Adams still remembered the phone call from Mike Thomas' mother in the morning. She wanted to ask about it but didn't know how to bring it up.

Instead, it reminded her of something she had long forgotten - the jewelry in the red packet and the photos! She had completely forgotten about them. At first, she was just thrilled to see Mike Thomas again, and then she enjoyed being with him so much that she didn't even remember those things. If she hadn't seen Mike Thomas answer a call from his family today, she might have never remembered.

She suddenly sat up and said to Mike Thomas, "Oh, I just remembered! I forgot to tell you! I found a package earlier, and it might be yours. There are your photos in it too. Let me show you! Just wait a moment!"

Thinking that the items were valuable, she had put them in the drawer where she normally kept precious things and found them immediately.

Mike Thomas took the red packet from Violet Adams and she glanced at his expression, which seemed normal and even a bit curious. So, does that mean it's not his?

Once he saw the contents of the packet clearly, Mike Thomas' eyes flickered for a moment, then he chuckled and said to Violet Adams, "Oh, I remember now. I had a streak of bad luck for a while, and my mom sent me this saying it could bring good luck but also bad luck. But I'm not superstitious, so I didn't really pay attention to whether I lost it or not. Now, it seems you've found it! You really are my good luck charm!"

Violet Adams felt that something was off about this explanation, but she didn't dwell on it and simply said, "Well, you should take it back then. It looks quite valuable."

She was just saying it casually. After all, returning lost items to their owners was a normal thing to do. Unexpectedly, Mike Thomas immediately turned serious and said forcefully, "No!"

Violet Adams was startled by his gloomy expression. As if realizing that his attitude was wrong. Mike Thomas quickly softened his expression and reached out to hold Violet Adams beside him.

He gently stroked her shoulder and patiently explained, "What's the difference between us now? I have plans to marry you in the future. Why should there be any distinction between mine and yours? I would be upset if you treat it as an outsider! Just keep it with you. You found it, so you are my little lucky charm! They should belong to you, right, baby?"

By the end of his words, his voice became soft and clingy, with a strong hint of playfulness. He then kissed Violet Adams' cheek. After being coaxed like this, Violet Adams couldn't maintain her seriousness.

She didn't dwell on the fact that the man had given her a stern look earlier. There's bound to be some friction between couples. In fact, occasional minor conflicts and arguments were normal. She had a relaxed mindset, thinking that maybe the man was upset because she and him were too clear about their financial situation. She wanted to ease his heart and put the items away again.

When he saw her putting the red packet back into the drawer, Mike Thomas finally broke into a big, bright smile and kissed her again. He happily suggested, "We finally have a day off today. Let's play a game together in the afternoon?"

Violet Adams naturally agreed. They both played the same mobile game, and they had developed some tacit understanding recently. They always cooperated well and had a lot of fun playing the game, which was a small relaxation from their busy work.

The game time flew by, and night gradually fell. When the final game notification ended, they realized they had idled away the whole afternoon.

Violet Adams was about to get up to cook when she looked at her Mike Thomas lying on the couch, his expression seemed inexplicably gloomy in the shadows. But Violet Adams didn't notice it.

Until they finished dinner and put down their knives and forks, Mike Thomas suddenly said to Violet Adams, "Baby, my mom called this morning and asked if I had a girlfriend. I told her the truth, and then she started urging me to get married... It's always like this, she calls and asks if I have a girlfriend, and when I do, she starts pressuring me to get married. It's really annoying, but my mom has been in poor health, so I don't dare to upset her too much. Although it's sudden and maybe too fast... After all, we have only confirmed our relationship not long ago. But I still want to ask, baby, would you be willing to cooperate with me and give my mom some comfort? It's not actually getting married, just going through a ceremony, like playing house... She's a bit confused in her mind, but she will surely think that we are really getting married. It would bring her some solace..."

Violet Adams stopped her hand from collecting the dishes. Her initial thought was absurdity, but as she listened further, she remembered the day they first spoke, when he mentioned going home because his family was unwell. It must have been his mom.

If... if it's just playing house... it shouldn't be a big deal, right?

She hesitated a bit...

Chapter 20

After clarifying Mike Thomas's specific plan, she relaxed and no longer felt so nervous.

If it's just pretending to get married in his relative's villa, without even having anyone as a witness, at most having the maid help take a photo, treating it as an artistic photo shoot, Violet Adams didn't really see any reason to refuse.

Mike Thomas sounded so serious, she thought he really wanted to have a mock wedding and host a reception. At the very least, she expected them to get a fake marriage certificate or something. It turned out none of that was necessary, and that put her mind at ease.

The two of them agreed on this plan, and in the evening, Mike Thomas went back home instead of staying at Violet Adams's place.

Although they were deeply in love, staying overnight was normal, but with work the next day, they were afraid of having sex, which would definitely result in being late for work.

When he was leaving, Mike Thomas seemed a bit reluctant, but there was no way around it. Violet Adams had to comfort him with several kisses, promising to make him fuck her next time, and only then he left satisfied.

The next weekend arrived quickly, on the same day off.

Violet Adams sat somewhat uneasily in Mike Thomas's car. Today, they were going to his relative's villa together. It was said that everything they needed was already prepared there, but she felt like it might be a bit exaggerated to borrow someone else's house. Maybe it would be fine to just go to a photography museum and take some wedding photos?

Suddenly, Violet Adams realized that it was all about the photos, and there was no need to strictly follow this process!

She shared her thoughts with Mike Thomas, but he reassured her nonchalantly, "It's fine. They're close relatives, so there's no need to feel embarrassed. Besides, they are not at home lately, and since we're here... I also want to go through this process with you. Don't you think it's romantic? The bridal chamber and candlelight night..." His words trailed off with a hint of longing. Violet Adams couldn't pretend to be clueless anymore.

She gave Mike Thomas a glare but, hearing his words, her heart began to anticipate it as well.

Mike Thomas glanced at the rearview mirror, his expression filled with satisfaction and meaning.

Mike Thomas's relative's villa was located in the outskirts, about a three-hour drive from where they lived. So they set off early in the morning and finally arrived at their destination just before noon. They had taken a day off specifically for this occasion, making sure to be fully prepared.

"Wow! This house is so remote!"

But at least this detached villa looked very beautiful. It had three floors and a large bamboo grove behind it. The only downside was that it was too close to the mountains, and the nearby houses were just some local people's homes, quite far away.

"There's nothing I can do. My relative is a local here, and this land belongs to him. But it's too far for anyone to come and cultivate, so they just built a house here. The family occasionally stays here during the scorching summer as a retreat. It's quite cool here."

As Mike Thomas explained, he parked the car in the yard and took Violet Adams to knock on the door.

A middle-aged man wearing a black suit, resembling an outfit from the olden days, opened the door. His face was sickly and pale, devoid of any emotions.

Violet Adams suddenly felt her heart skip a beat when she met his lifeless eyes. She even instinctively held onto her boyfriend's arm. He patted her hand, smiled reassuringly at her, and then spoke to the man, saying, "Uncle Milo, we have arrived."

That man nod and then opened the door wider to let them in.

The interior decoration was very luxurious, one could say it was magnificent. While Violet Adams internally criticized the taste of the owners, she was stunned by the flowers and the white silk hanging all over the room.

They were only supposed to go through the motions, so why make such a big fuss... It seemed too exaggerated.

This wasn't even the most exaggerated part. When they entered the master bedroom and saw the room arranged as a proper bridal chamber, Violet Adams was taken aback. She tugged at Mike Thomas's sleeve, wearing a conflicted expression, and said, "Isn't it... strange to use someone else's master bedroom for this? And the homeowners actually agreed?!"

Mike Thomas turned to look at her, and for a moment, she felt as if she was being stared at by something terrifying. But when she snapped out of it, she realized that it was simply the gentle and reassuring look from Mike Thomas. She brushed it off as a result of not getting enough sleep.

Mike Thomas cupped her face and expressed his tender affection, saying, "My Violet, you're so considerate! But don't think too much about it. Our family and this relative's family have a very close relationship, and all of this has been arranged in advance by them. It's natural for them to be willing."

Then, he leaned down and whispered softly in Violet Adams's ear, "Don't dwell on these thoughts. Just treat it as an immersive game. Don't you think it would be exciting to wear wedding attire?"

Violet Adams couldn't help but be frustrated with her boyfriend, who was consumed by thoughts of sex. But she had chosen him as her dream guy, so what could she do? She could only indulge him...

So, miraculously, Violet Adams accepted this setting. Soon after, someone came to call them for lunch. It was a young man wearing a black suit, said to be Uncle Milo's son. His face had a different shade of pale red compared to Uncle Milo's.

Mike Thomas explained that the young man wanted the wedding to be more festive and not as rigid as the older generation.

That's what he said... Violet Adams looked at the two identical faces devoid of expression with a sickly pale gray color, and then looked at the two reddish spots on Uncle Milo's son's face. She couldn't help but feel that there wasn't much joyousness in sight...

After they finished their meal, they went upstairs to rest together because Violet Adams felt tired and sleepy from not sleeping well last night and not getting to sleep in the morning. And of course, Mike Thomas had to accompany her.

It was only when they were away from the others downstairs that Violet Adams felt a sense of relief. It was strange to be constantly stared at by someone with an expressionless face while eating, but seeing Mike Thomas eating naturally without saying anything, she didn't complain.

They took a nap in another room. In Mike Thomas's words, they could only sleep in the bridal chamber bed after the ceremonial formalities in the evening.

This explanation sounded very strange. It was clearly just a formality to give comfort to Mike Thomas's mother, so why did Mike Thomas seem so engrossed in it... Was he taking it too seriously?

Although she found it strange, Violet Adams approached the matter with the mindset of "since I'm here... let's treat it as role-playing." It didn't feel as off to her anymore. She and Mike Thomas took a peaceful nap together without any disturbances.

After waking up, the two of them played around in bed for a while, and eventually, Mike Thomas initiated intimate activities, taking advantage of the fact that there was nobody at home and the servants wouldn't disturb them. He didn't feel the slightest bit sorry for himself and thoroughly enjoyed himself with Violet Adams.

On the contrary, Violet Adams's face turned red with embarrassment. Having sex in someone else's house always made her feel uneasy, although Mike Thomas seemed completely unfazed...

Chapter 21

The two of them played around for a while, and when it was almost time, Mike Thomas took Violet Adams to the mistress's dressing room where the bridal gowns were already prepared.

Violet Adams changed her clothes there, while Mike Thomas needed to put on his black suit. When he appeared in front of her wearing the red and black groom's attire, Violet Adams's eyes showed amazement.

Mike Thomas also looked at her tenderly. With her hair down, the golden strands intertwined with the white dress, she looked more captivating than ever.

After they changed their clothes, it was already dusk. Uncle Milo and his son were waiting at the door. They followed behind Mike Thomas and Violet Adams, with a camera in one hand and a tray in the other, holding two rings.

With layers of white veil and flowers, the two walked hand in hand towards the hall. Before entering the ballroom, Violet Adams heard the wedding march playing inside.

I finally found someone
Who knocks me off my feet
I finally found the one
Who makes me feel complete
It started over coffee
We started out as friends
It's funny how from simple things
The best things begin
This time is different
It's all because of you

After the two of them stood still in the hall, the music stopped, and Uncle Milo spoke with a stiff voice, "We gather here in the presence of God to celebrate the wedding of groom Mike Thomas and bride Violet

Adams, and to pray for the grace of our Heavenly Father. Marriage is the most precious bond in morality, ordained by God and blessed by the Lord. It is a significant event in life and should not be taken lightly. It should be approached with respect and piety, honoring God's will."

Then Uncle Milo twitched his expressionless pale-gray face and continued, "Mike Thomas, do you take this woman, Violet Adams, to be your lawful wedded wife, to live together forever?"

Mike Thomas immediately replied, "I do."

The stiff voice resounded again, "Violet Adams, do you take this man, Mike Thomas, to be your lawful wedded husband, to live together forever?"

Although it was just a pretend marriage, Violet Adams sweetly answered, "I do."

Uncle Milo continued with a stiff voice, "Now, I invite the couple to recite their wedding vows."

Uncle Milo's son handed them the note cards with the wedding vows written on them. Mike Thomas held Violet Adams's hand with his right hand, gazing at her tenderly, and recited, "Entreat me not to leave you, or to return from following after you, For where you go I will go, and where you stay I will stay. Your people will be my people, and your God will be my God. And where you die, I will die and there I will be buried. May the Lord do with me and more if anything but death parts you from me."

Violet Adams was still immersed in his gentle gaze and did not hear what he recited until Mike Thomas gently squeezed her hand, making her realize that it was her turn.

Violet Adams looked at the note card and began to recite, "Entreat me not to leave you, or to return from following after you, For where you go I will go, and where you stay I will stay. Your people will be my people, and your God will be my God..."

Then she paused and looked at Mike Thomas with a puzzled and astonished expression. It was just a formality, why did they have to make such serious vows? It made it seem like they were actually getting married.

Mike Thomas embraced her tightly, his eyes filled with tenderness, and whispered in her ear, "Darling, it's just a formality. It doesn't matter what the vows say, just recite them as instructed. I already recited the same vows just now."

Violet Adams continued to recite, "And where you die, I will die and there I will be buried. May the Lord do with me and more if anything but death parts you from me."

When she finished, Mike Thomas smiled meaningfully.

Then Uncle Milo continued with a stiff voice, "Now, I invite the groom and bride to exchange rings."

After they put the rings on each other's fingers, the stiff voice continued, "Oh Lord, may these rings serve as a symbol of everlasting love and unity. Amen. Alright, groom, you may now kiss your wife."

Mike Thomas planted a deep kiss on Violet Adams's lips.

At the same time, the clock in the hall chimed, its resonant chimes seemed to strike at Violet Adams's heart. She was being led by Mike Thomas towards the master bedroom, their bridal chamber, but she felt her legs growing heavier and her whole body feeling light and airy.

She had a vague feeling that something was off, but she couldn't figure out what it was... Until she sat on the bridal bed and looked up at the familiar yet unfamiliar man in front of her. She saw him hand her a glass of wine and, with a smile, wrap his wrist around hers, both of them holding their wine glasses. She brought the glass to her lips, took a sip, but tears instantly welled up in her eyes.

She understood, but it was already too late. All the illogical details flashed in her mind in that instant, and she had already guessed what had happened to her. Even during the ceremony, she couldn't move her body, as if someone invisible was supporting her, guiding her through the entire process.

Her heart ached, why... After deceiving her for so long, why did he choose this moment to let her discover the truth...

She couldn't utter any words, only tears streaming from her eyes, pleadingly looking at the groom in front of her. Although she knew it was impossible, seeing his tender gaze, a faintly impossible hope arose in her heart.

What if he loved her and spared her when he saw her begging? She was still so young, she didn't want to die. Her parents had only her as their child, what would they do if she died... and all because of this...

Even if she wasn't superstitious, considering what she had experienced, she probably knew that the object she had found didn't just have a lucky charm effect as Mike Thomas claimed.

The man's face remained as clear as ever, his perfect porcelain-like features filled with tenderness for the woman in front of him. He sat on the edge of the bed, gently caressing her tear-stained face, softly whispering, "This is our bridal night, Violet. From today onwards, you are my bride. Are you unhappy? We love each other so deeply, we will definitely be together forever. It's such a pity that I didn't get to know you while I was alive, but fortunately, fate allowed me to have you after death. Violet, I truly, truly love you..."

Mike Thomas embraced her, repeatedly expressing his love. From hope to despair, it only took a few minutes. Ever since the ceremony, she had been trapped. There was no escape...

"Sleep, my darling. When you wake up, everything will be fine..."

With the fading sound of a male voice, Violet Adams slowly lost consciousness.

Story Four: Demon's Love and Sex

Chapter 22

In a brightly lit interrogation room, a woman dressed in a high-end custom-made silk fishtail dress had her hands handcuffed behind the chair. Her long hair flowed like a waterfall, and her delicate skin was almost translucent. Her pair of white and smooth legs were wrapped in a tight-fitting skirt, exposing only her enticing calves. She had lightly applied makeup on her exquisite face, with slender and upturned eyes that seemed to be able to snatch away a person's soul with just a casual glance. Even in this restrained state, she showed no sign of embarrassment.

She glanced around at the people gathered around her with a half-smile, observing their eyes filled with disgust or fear. Instead of feeling angry, she closed her eyes and savored their emotions with great interest.

Taking a deep breath, she couldn't help but admire in her heart: Oh... this is the taste, the hatred and boredom emanating from humans, hmm... and even a hint of desire... They were all her food!

When she opened her eyes again, they were blood-red, with no trace of white.

A tall and sharp-looking woman in a gray trench coat raised her arm upon seeing this scene and said coldly, "Everyone, step back! Don't let this spider demon bewitch your minds!"

The others snapped out of their momentary confusion and took a few steps back, all watching the woman on the chair with vigilant eyes.

"This demon is indeed powerful. Just now, I felt completely unable to control my own body!"

"Yes! Everyone, be careful. We don't know what other tricks demon has besides manipulating minds. Don't fall into her trap."

The woman's pupils had returned to normal by now. She chuckled, her voice charming and alluring, but her words made the faces of those present change.

"What a joke. I only amplified the dark side within your hearts. As for not being able to control your bodies, it's about not being able to control your own shafts...Humans are truly hypocritical."

The woman with short hair turned her head abruptly and looked at the two men who had spoken earlier. As expected, their lower bodies had already pitched a tent, a stark contrast to their earlier righteous words.

The woman with short hair clenched her teeth in anger. Her eyes narrowed, and with a trembling hand, she picked up a whip that suddenly appeared in her hand and lashed it beside the restrained woman. Dust was kicked up from the ground, and even though it was made of concrete, it had been marked deeply by the terrifying force, a clear testament to the fury of the whip-wielder.

But this whip did not intimidate the audacious spider demon. The spider demon still held some disdain in her heart, not wanting to admit that she had been caught so easily by this group of people. It was truly embarrassing.

Thinking about this, her face darkened inexplicably, and a hint of red anger flickered in her eyes. Her gaze turned to the man who had been silently leaning against the wall and playing with his phone since he entered. Today, he was wearing a wrinkled white shirt, clearly of cheap quality. The wrinkles on it made him look like he had been haphazardly thrown into a washing machine, taken out to dry under the sun, and then stiffened into a deeply wrinkled piece, like a dried-up and wrinkled pickle.

There was a big hole on one leg of his jeans. She knew that it was a trendy style of ripped jeans popular among modern young humans. His brown messy hair blocked his eyes due to his head-lowered posture, but she knew that his gaze must have been utterly bored fish-eyes. She still remembered the look in his eyes when he bound her with his magic, as if he was saying, 'Is this small shrimp worth my effort? Let's finish quickly! I really want to go off work...'

Damn it! This made her even angrier than being caught!

She suddenly curled her lips into a smile and said to the few people in front of her, who were acting as if they were facing a great enemy, "Didn't you want to know what I have done? This story is quite long... Do you want to hear it?"

Chapter 23

When it comes to the people she has harmed...how can you say it's harm? Aren't these things consensual? It was probably about a thousand years ago, in a dynasty that has long been lost to history...

The spider demon's name was Flower Black. As she was a black spider, so she made her surname Black, and she thought she was as beautiful as a flower, so her name was Flower. Although she didn't have much education, the name sounded quite fitting to her aesthetics, so she grew to like the name she chose for herself even more.

There's not much deep meaning to it, but it sounds nice and looks good, and she is very satisfied with it.

However, there were always a few self-proclaimed talented scholars who looked down upon her name when they got close to her, considering it too explicit and frivolous, not matching her.

What a joke, if they weren't frivolous, would they have engaged with her without any formalities? At that time, she wasn't just a woman in the brothels, she even pretended to be from a respectable family. Clearly, those men weren't a good persons, but they thought they already had an intimate relationship, so they could speak freely and intervene, only to be carried to bed by her a few times and moan while sucking her dry, the talented scholars who boasted their talents by saying "even dying under the peony flowers is romantic", truly laughable.

Not every man who had relations with her would end up dead, after all, she wasn't a bad demon. Only those with inherent problems or those who did something that displeased her would have their spiritual energy sucked dry by her. Come to think of it, she was actually doing a good deed. In order to prevent these people from harming truly innocent young women, she had to be proactive and uphold justice.

During the time of doing good deeds, she had also encountered a few different men.

The first one was... um... She didn't know which year's top scholar he was. Flower Red at that time particularly favored this kind of handsome and elegant-looking yet reserved and virtuous scholar, but in reality, all the supposedly virtuous men she had encountered before were actually false purity. Some people had impeccable reputations, but in reality, they had several concubines at home, and their private parts were worn thin like needles. They still pretended to be virtuous, which was sickening to witness.

But the top scholar, Devin Brown, was different. He was genuinely virtuous, born into a poor farmer's family, and knew from a young age exactly what he wanted. The trajectory of his growth wasn't smooth sailing; it was filled with all sorts of people and darkness. In order to fund his private studies, he even resorted to theft. There was nothing that could hinder him from achieving his goals, including useless women.

Of course, he was successful. His early experiences taught him how to wear a "mask" that would increase the favor of others. He always appeared calm and composed, as if nothing could surprise him, with a clear and pure demeanor. Together with his perfect appearance, anyone who looked at him would only praise his gentlemanly qualities.

After secretly investigating him, Flower Red, who thought he was to her liking, playfully wanted to see his true face change. She chose a dark and windy night and dropped herself into his bathtub while he was bathing.

The dark and smooth wooden tub undulated with the water, occasionally being scooped up by a hand that was as jade-like as it was distinct in its bony structure. The water would trickle down onto his well-built chest, and the droplets would then fall back into the tub, merging and dissipating with the others.

His brown hair foamed in the water, sticking to his back, forming an alluring pattern. And then, a large spider immediately descended, as if lured by it.

Yes, Flower Black jumped off with its true form and floated on the water surface, a purely black-legged large spider with a belly, suddenly dropped in front of the man and floated on the water surface in front of him. Its eyes were very small, and theoretically he shouldn't have noticed it, but he felt like they made eye contact and even blinked... Do spiders have eyelids?

Devin Brown, who had always remained calm no matter what he encountered, had his expression cracked in that instant.

Chapter 24

How interesting it was to see the man, initially startled by the spider, calm down upon seeing it transform into a human-like figure. Should this be considered calm? After all, his expression quickly turned back to being emotionless. He didn't pay any attention to the enchanting woman suddenly appearing in the bathtub and spilling water all over the floor. He calmly finished his bath, got up from the tub, dried his body, put on his underwear, and walked towards the inner bedroom without giving her a second glance.

As for Flower Black, she found it amusing to be ignored. Men who had encountered her in the past were either captivated by her appearance or scared to unconsciousness by her true form. It was the first time she had met a supernatural being showing such composure. He didn't even spare her a second look.

She held her face up to the remaining hot water in the tub, feeling incredibly beautiful. So she also got up and floated towards the inner room.

By the time she entered, the man was already half-lying on the bed, holding a book in his hand. His expression under the lamp looked somewhat cold, in stark contrast to his gentle appearance when he was on the horse earlier in the day.

She gently smiled and floated down next to him. With a wave of her hand, the blanket lifted, revealing a soft bed with a comfortable mattress and a faint fragrance. It seemed fresh, as if it had just been changed.

She pressed herself against the man's warm body, leaning against his shoulder and exhaled a fragrant breath, "It's getting late. Why don't we rest?"

It seemed like he couldn't ignore her anymore. He put down the book in his hand, turned his head, and asked coldly, "What do you want?"

He must be angry. Finally reaching this point, he thought there would be no more surprises. He thought he could soon achieve his ambitions and make his dreams come true. But there are actually supernatural beings in this world? He felt like he had been hit hard in his heart, as if all his efforts were about to become a joke.

He never believed in ghosts or deities. Everything he had experienced since childhood had taught him that if he wanted something, he had to rely on himself. But if there are ghosts and supernatural beings in the world, what chance does a mortal have? Any random little fairy could take their lives, just like the spider demon currently embracing him in a disheveled state.

Unaware that she was being regarded as "any random little fairy," Flower Black innocently met his deep gaze and blinked.

"Why do you look at me like that? I have long admired your great name and admired your talent and handsomeness. I just wanted to spend the night with you, and enjoy ourselves..."

Being propositioned so straightforwardly for the first time, no... being propositioned so straightforwardly by a demon, Devin Brown paused for a second before coldly laughing.

"Is that so? I am afraid that after spending night together, it will be my time of death."

While he spoke of his own death, there was no trace of fear on his face. He looked at Flower Black as if she was already dead, devoid of emotions, chillingly cold.

Flower Black covered her lips and chuckled, her eyebrows and eyes enchanting.

"You seem to misunderstand me. I am not a wicked monster. life? I already said, I just desire your body... If you're not willing to sleep with me, it's OK. But you misunderstand me like this, it truly saddens me..."

Devin Brown remained unmoved. Looking at his cold and rigid face, Flower Black's heart thumped at that moment. This man! He was so handsome, imposing, and different from anyone she had met before.

She felt herself starting to be drawn to him. What would this kind of man look like when consumed by desire? Would he become ugly and repulsive? Thinking this, Flower Black became even more excited.

Since then, Flower Black moved into Devin Brown's house. Although the hosts were unwelcoming, she didn't care. Why would Flower Black need anyone's welcome? Besides the palace shrouded in dragon aura, there was nowhere she couldn't go. She believed that a mere mortal was just a bit more courageous, and in the end, they wouldn't be able to resist her seduction.

However, reality proved to be completely different from what she had imagined. He not only resisted her seduction but also, after spending some time together (being relentlessly pursued by her), learned how to completely ignore her.

Moreover, he was incredibly bold. He continued his duties at the Academy as usual and only allowed the servants to serve him when he returned home. He ate when it was time to eat and washed up and slept when it was time to do so, as if a beauty of this magnitude was just the air.

Flower Black couldn't help laughing with anger. She did use some deception, making everyone except Devin Brown unable to see her. But remember: everyone except Devin Brown could still see her.

However, once he discovered that she was using deception on the people around them, he began to blatantly ignore her. No method worked. Threats meant nothing to him, and kind words fell on deaf ears. He could even put on a gentle and charming demeanor while having a pleasant conversation with others.

Devin Brown wasn't a fool. If this demon wanted to kill him, she would have done so already, without the need to cling onto his house. Besides, if the demon truly wanted to kill him, he wouldn't be able to escape. Since it had come to this, he had accepted it. He no longer wanted to ponder the worthiness him doubt himself but also doubt the entire world.

That's how it went, Flower Black was never able to successfully seduce him. In the past, she didn't have to put much effort in, those well-dressed men would willingly come to her, and she could quickly make them her prey. But for the first time, encountering someone immune to her charms, Flower Black felt a sense of challenge arise within her.

So, for the first time, she did something she had never done before...she actively teased him with her body.

It was actually an impulsive act. Flower Black, at that time, was not as mature as she would be a thousand years later. She simply believed that all men were not good people, though she didn't know who had instilled this mindset in her or in what manner. It was deeply rooted in her, and she never questioned whether her selected target had any flaws. She believed that their dirty intentions were well-concealed and that one day she would catch them in the act. And when that time came, she wouldn't hesitate to devour them.

So she did something bold. Taking advantage of the distraction, while Devin Brown was entertaining his friend in the flower hall, she leaned against him and discreetly slipped her hand underneath his robe, using her delicate and nimble fingers to gently grip his yet-to-be-erect manhood, concealed by the warmth of the low table.

The hot and heavy cock grew under her touch, becoming harder, but his faint smile only wavered for a moment before returning to normal, and he continued conversing with his friend as if nothing had happened.

Flower Black half-heartedly listened to their conversation, which seemed like a discussion of political factions in the court. But their words were veiled and full of innuendos. After a few sentences, she became impatient with trying to understand their true meaning and focused solely on pleasing this man.

Chapter 25

In the indoor warmth of a winter day, with a brazier and a heated table, Devin Brown, being in his own home, naturally didn't wear too much. He only wore a black silk robe while playing chess with his friend. The woman next to him, unaffected by the cold, was even more extravagant. She wore a floor-length silk gown, with nothing underneath, baring her chest, and yet covered by several layers of sheer veils, partially visible yet hidden. But Devin Brown was accustomed to seeing women dressed like this all the time, although today was different. She actually disregarded the presence of others and directly started caressing him, which stirred a slight anger in his heart.

Taking advantage of the cover of the heated table, no one could see this seemingly dignified and pure man who was aroused. The woman's hand continued to intermittently stroke his imposing member, smearing the clear fluid that oozed from the tip all over, sometimes using her palm tenderly to support the two balls below, lightly closing her grip with one hand, as if playing with two round and smooth walnut pearls without friction or collision, just the touch of her palm against it. At other times, her hand moved slowly and ambiguously on the inside of his thigh, feeling the pulsation of his meridians.

Flower Black was busy for a while, but frustratingly, the man showed no reaction at all! Clearly, he was already aroused down there, but there was an obstacle preventing it from fully taking off. Despite her attempts to arouse him, he didn't embarrass himself on the spot. Could it be that her strong scent of lust didn't reach that idiot across from them? His friend was happily chatting while sporting an erect member. If this matter were discovered, regardless of whether it would become public knowledge or not, Flower Black wouldn't be as furious as she was now. But instead, when the man left, he only half-praised and half-admonished him, saying, "Devin, I think the fragrance in this hall is quite strong. Although incense is good, using too much might hinder others. Perhaps you should use less?"

Prior to this, Devin Brown had faked a cough a few times, claiming that he might have caught a slight cold, so he didn't get up to see his friend off. His friend knew him well and understood that he wasn't an unreasonable person, so why would he mind such a trivial matter? But when he smelled the increasingly fragrant scent in the hall, he couldn't help but offer some advice. Little did he know that it wasn't just some incense, but the aroma of debauchery permeating the entire room.

Mixed in the heated air, the intoxicating scent, like the fragrance of flowers, could not possibly just be emanating from Devin Brown. He simply smiled and nodded, agreeing with his friend's reminder, "Yes, I used a bit too much this time. I will definitely pay attention next time. Thank you for reminding me, Eric."

Once his friend left, his expression turned cold, and he firmly grasped the hand that was still causing mischief between his groin and pulled the woman away from him.

"Oh... Why do you treat me so rudely? Haven't I served you well?" The woman feigned a dramatic fall to the ground and whimpered.

The man was not as enraged as she had expected; instead, he smirked coldly, his voice icy with a hint of elusive mockery. He even casually poured himself a cup of coffee.

"You still have the nerve to talk about this? Perhaps you should first smell yourself, the scent of your lust is so strong that even my departing friend could smell it."

Flower Black froze, in disbelief she reached down to confirm, and unsurprisingly found her hand sticky.

Wide-eyed in disbelief, she wondered why the man couldn't smell the man's bodily fluids, only to realize she had unknowingly masked the scent herself! As she fondled and played with this deceitful and treacherous man's cock, she realized she had already become wet!

Annoyed and embarrassed, her body gradually became transparent, and her shocked and angry face, as well as her beautiful female form, disappeared on the spot.

Thinking of the expression of frustration and anger the woman had before disappearing, a pleasant chuckle suddenly echoed in the room.

The man's eyes still held a hint of amusement. Ever since the woman began frequenting his presence, he had already established new rules for his subordinates. At this moment, he didn't call anyone, nor would any foolish subordinate dare to come in. Therefore, he unabashedly opened his robe, the belt already loosened by the enchantress, and revealed the rock-hard manhood manipulated by the woman.

This member was not perfectly straight but curved like a goose's neck. It was slightly bent, but just enough to effortlessly graze the sensitive area of the woman's mound with a casual thrust. When touched, it felt scorching hot, seeming to scald one's very soul. It was simultaneously hard and thick, making Flower Black, who had seen many cocks, unable to resist. That's also why her desire had uncontrollably caused her to become wet after just a brief touch.

She couldn't help but imagine how it would feel to have this extraordinary member thrust into her core. It seemed within her reach, as if she could devour it with her own eager entrance. This was something she refused to admit - she was the first one to feel desire, not the desire to consume him, but rather a carnal desire.

At that moment, she was lying beside the man, invisible and enjoying the sight of a handsome man pleasuring himself. It must be said, he was truly an exceptional man who aroused a desire for the demon to dominate...

The man found it quite amusing too. Of course, he knew the spider demon hadn't left; who knows, maybe she was watching nearby. But so what?

In his mind, he imagined the other's flushed cheeks from anger and those occasional glimpses of true character revealed in their eyes, his hand movements neither rushed nor slow. Even though his member was continuously leaking, he didn't hasten his actions. He simply slid his hand slowly up and down the shaft, with great patience, like an experienced hunter setting a trap. Before capturing the prey, one must patiently wait and occasionally give them a taste of sweetness.

Flower Black was becoming frantic, wishing she could help him relieve himself. At this moment, she didn't even know her own thoughts. She didn't want him to continue teasing her with his slow manipulation of the increasingly colored shaft in front of her eyes, nor did she want him to bring her to climax after a few strokes. Her legs involuntarily rubbed against each other, like a slow swimming seductive serpent. Drips of her arousal seeped through the fabric of her skirt, staining the ground, intensifying the aroma in the room.

She didn't notice the slight movement of the man's nostrils, nor did she realize his smile deepening in his eyes. She was unaware that he had already guessed she hadn't left and was carefully watching his every move. As she swallowed her saliva, she berated herself for being so weak-willed.

The man lightly flicked the shiny glans a few times with his fingertips. When he lifted his hand, several long strands of desire connected his fingertips to the urethral opening. His finger hovered above the tip of his member, waiting for the strands to snap before descending upon the glans again. That momentary sensation made him involuntarily moan with pleasure.

In his mind, he imagined the woman's expression at this moment, and his mood became even better. Although on the surface, he appeared calm and content, he spent a full hour playing with himself before finally reaching climax.

Flower Black was still silently cursing the man in her heart, frustrated that he seemed to be enjoying himself for so long. But then, the man suddenly changed positions and ejaculated onto her clothes and face. Subconsciously, she licked her lips and tasted the faint metallic scent mixed with the man's unique fragrance. She was stunned.

Chapter 26

In the following days, Flower Black did not appear in front of the man, and Devin Brown had no knowledge of the incident where he accidentally ejaculated onto the spider demon's face. He simply thought he had angered her that day, but whether she appeared or not had no actual effect on him.

Although Flower Black's anger towards him didn't linger in his mind for more than two seconds, she still didn't want to kill him. So she continued to stay hidden and followed the man around every day, observing his every move.

She couldn't explain why she was doing this, but she had silently observed him for almost half a month.

She found that the man lived a disciplined and boring life, strict with himself but lenient with others. No matter what others did, as long as it didn't affect his own interests, even if someone stood in front of him and called him a hypocrite, he would simply smile and not get angry.

The present emperor seemed diligent, attending the early morning court sessions every day. He would wake up at three in the morning, and even after finishing his official duties, he would continue to read or write. Occasionally, when he was in a good mood, he would paint a few paintings or invite friends over for wine and chess. This kind of life was utterly predictable, and for Flower Black, it was extremely boring.

Although she felt bored inside, her body still faithfully followed him every day. Even when he went to the palace, she would sit under the corridor where he usually sat, set up his chessboard, and play against herself. She would check the time and get the feeling that he was about to come back, so she would quickly put the chessboard away and pretend she wasn't there.

Another month passed, and she started feeling increasingly bored. However, for some reason, she still didn't want to reveal herself in front of him. Why was she angry with him in the first place?

She couldn't remember clearly, but it didn't really matter. She put the black chess pieces back into the chess jar and rested her chin on her hand, watching raindrops fall from the eaves like broken strings. The sound of the dripping rain didn't cause a ripple in her heart. She thought to herself, maybe it's time to leave.

While Flower Black was contemplating leaving, Devin Brown suddenly returned early and caught her in the act. Watching the invisible hand mercilessly throw each chess piece into the jar, his mouth twitched, and a sense of speechlessness surged within him. At the same time, deep down, he strangely felt relieved. Had she not left yet?

As if sensing his presence, the white chess pieces paused in the air before pretending nothing happened and landing on the chessboard. The air fell silent, with only the sound of dripping raindrops.

Devin Brown sat across from the chessboard. He had been busy lately and rarely had such leisurely moments. He picked up a chess piece with his jade-like fingers and placed it on the board. Accompanied by the sound of the piece landing, he said, "Come out, I know you're here."

The air remained silent. Flower Black looked at the man in front of her with a strange expression, feeling that his aura was becoming more settled. She knew that the political arena was a place that polished individuals, but was this evolution a little too fast?

Seeing no response, the man looked somewhat helpless, "Don't be angry anymore. It's been so long. Shouldn't your anger have dissipated by now?"

Flower Black thought for a moment and realized she wasn't angry anymore... She had even forgotten why she was angry in the first place because the impression of him ejaculating on her face overshadowed everything that had happened before, yet he remained oblivious.

The calmness that had gradually settled in Flower Black's heart was suddenly overwhelmed by a sense of grievance. She felt that she couldn't just leave and let this man off so easily! So, Devin Brown saw a graceful female figure slowly appear on the other side of the chessboard.

She was still wearing the silky long dress, but with a different style, without the cloak concealing her. The translucent fabric hugged her chest tightly, revealing half of her smooth and worryingly fragile-looking fair skin. The fabric was somewhat see-through, and her rosy nipples were teasingly visible through the veil. Paired with her alluringly innocent face, Devin Brown immediately became aroused.

"Do you know that you came on my face that day!"

The woman had a serious expression on her face, standing tall with her large breasts. She dropped a bombshell as soon as she opened her mouth. Devin Brown had to retract his gaze from admiring the view and recalled which day she was referring to. It was somewhat absurd and coincidental. He thought that at most, she was just watching from the sidelines. Who could have imagined that they were so close to each other and in such a position...

Although he hadn't witnessed it himself, Devin Brown quickly flashed through that scene in his mind and immediately acknowledged it. He kindly admitted, "It was my fault. So, what do you want?"

Flower Black, on the other hand, seemed prepared for this. She gave a cunning smile and answered, "I want you to do whatever I say! Start by touching yourself like you did that day, and show it to me!"

Devin Brown reluctantly agreed with a bitter smile, wearing an expression of helplessness and unwillingness all over his face. He said to Flower Black with a bit of shameful endurance, "How about we go to the bed then..."

Flower Black enjoyed his reluctance, and her mood suddenly improved. She thought to herself, how could she not have control over this mere mortal! So, she generously agreed to his request.

At this point, Flower Black was no longer thinking about leaving. She felt incredibly confident after witnessing his performance, and she no longer found it boring. She even thought that if she could see this man's helpless and powerless face every day, she would be willing to build a nest in this mansion!

She followed behind the man as they walked along the corridor, not forgetting to remind him to bring the chessboard. As the man picked up the chessboard and the jar, he had a slightly inexplicable expression on his face, as if he had thought of something interesting. However, Flower Black, who didn't notice his current expression, just felt a shiver down her spine for some unknown reason.

She touched her own silk dress and wondered if it was because she had been neglecting her cultivation recently that she suddenly felt a chill. Her expression became solemn, and in her heart, she made a determination to start cultivating diligently from now on!

The two stepped into the man's bedroom, the sky outside still appearing bright, but the light inside became dimmer after closing the door. The man didn't turn on the lights, but Flower Black didn't mind. The gaze of a demon was different from that of a human, and she laughed in her heart, believing that Devin Brown must be ashamed and didn't want to turn on the lights, thinking it would obstruct her vision. How naive! He dared to masturbate in the hall that day, but now he didn't even dare to turn on the lights, what a coward!

However... thinking about it, Flower Black suddenly became more calm and realized that something didn't seem right. Was Devin Brown that kind of person? Would he be too afraid to turn on the lights because he was scared of being seen by her?

Chapter 27

Without giving Flower Black more time to think, the man had already taken off the lining of his belt, leaving only a loose robe, with nothing else underneath.

Flower Black turned her gaze and stared at the man's solid and well-defined abs, unable to resist reaching out and touching those enticing abdominal muscles.

His cock had already risen, and the man sat on the edge of the bed, his hands leaning back and supporting himself on the bed, allowing the nearby demoness to explore his body. The robe hung on either side, not providing any cover, but instead being mischievously pulled up by the demoness, hanging on the man's erect cock, creating an imposing tent.

Having touched the man's abs enough, Flower Black moved downwards and teasingly rubbed his black pubic hair, then grabbed his hot and thick shaft. She played with it a few times, but suddenly felt that something was off. She raised her head and ordered the man, "You touch it yourself and let me watch!"

The man didn't refuse her and obediently grasped his own shaft with one hand. He then slowly began stroking and fondling it, as if he was quite accustomed to this slow speed. The wrist moved the shaft up and down in a smooth motion, with the glans being teased subtly, gradually oozing clear fluid that made the head glisten. When the liquid dripped, he patiently used his index finger to coat the entire shaft with the dripping lustful fluid, massaging and rubbing it as if giving a massage, occasionally letting out sexy moans and low whimpers.

Flower Black was somewhat entranced watching, amazed at how skilled this man was, even more so than herself! Unknowingly, her inner thighs had already become soaked, dropping with droplets of fragrance-laden lustful fluid, along with the intoxicating scent of blossoms filling the room. This time, she didn't just stand by and watch like the last time.

Unable to resist being seduced by the man's self-pleasure, she ordered him to stop and instructed him to place his hands back behind him. And then, on impulse, she buried her head and licked the red glans once, tasting the tangy secretion with a hint of fragrance. A tingling sensation ran through her, and she inwardly cursed the man for being so seductive, even though she continued lavishly bathing his shaft with her saliva.

Devin Brown watched as the demoness pleasured him under him, a growing smile in his eyes. Feeling pleasured himself, he couldn't help but occasionally let out low moans, and sometimes he purposely thrust his hips a few times to make his shaft penetrate deeper. Once, he pushed it into Flower Black's throat, and her contracting throat caused his shaft to be squeezed momentarily, nearly unable to resist the urge to forcefully fuck her. However, when she raised her teary-eyed head, he changed to an expression of both guilt and shame, unable to control his lower body.

Flower Black was repeatedly bewildered by his behavior, as if he had returned to his harmless and polite appearance in front of others, ignoring the fact that his pulsating veins were becoming more ferocious beneath being pleasured.

The floral fragrance in the room had become overwhelming, and Flower Black's chest couldn't bear the weight of her large breasts, causing her blouse to open up. Devin Brown looked on with admiration, feeling regretful that he couldn't touch them at the moment, so he could only let them be lonely for a while longer.

However, Flower Black didn't pay attention to all of this. The premium shaft she had been longing for was right in front of her, so naturally, she wanted to taste it first. She had the man lie flat on the bed, his cock standing high, and she gently caressed the curve of his erect member, giving it a slight support before lifting her hips and sitting down on it.

"Oh... it's so long, so big! It's hitting me! This angle... Oh... truly perfect..."

Chapter 28

As soon as the cock entered her hole, it began to push in on its own. The thick shaft got stuck right at the entrance, causing a feeling of fullness that couldn't be accommodated. The throbbing glans brushed over her sensitive area, arousing intense sensations. But this spider demon was greedy. With both hands on the man's abs, she eagerly attempted to swallow the entire shaft.

Seeing her eager expression, the man's face twitched, as if saying, "I can't resist you, so I'll help you." In an instant, Flower Black felt a sense of impending doom. As expected, the next moment, the man reached out and held her slender waist, pressing down forcefully.

"Wait!! Wait... Oh... Ugh... You foul man, you're so deep... Oh... It hurts..."

Tears welled up in Flower Black's eyes as the cock poked at her, and amidst the pain, a hint of pleasure emerged. The hot and warm intrusion felt like her pussy was being heated all over, creating an indescribable sense of satisfaction. Her pussy involuntarily contracted and squeezed, wishing to swallow the entire shaft. Nonetheless, she still had her wits about her. She knew that this man was different from the others, and she didn't want to end his life.

Once she felt seated comfortably, the man supported her waist and began thrusting upward. Flower Black was being thrust so hard that her lower abdomen quivered, her pussy tingled, and her large breasts bounced up and down. It wasn't until he grabbed her nipples that she realized it wasn't supposed to be about her being in control anymore. How did it become her being dominated by him?

Helpless as her pussy and legs went numb, she couldn't summon any strength to resist. She was like a mortal woman who had been thoroughly fucked by a man, only able to hang on his body, her hands gripping his shoulders for support. Meanwhile, his cock relentlessly pounded inside her, creating splashing waves at the point where their genitals met.

After thrusting for a while, Devin Brown noticed the woman had become limp from his fucking. He became less restrained and lifted her up, inserting his cock into her again, repeatedly and forcefully. The slightly curved angle of his shaft scraped against all her sensitive spots with each motion, causing her to moan loudly and crave more.

"I've hit the spot... Just as I expected... Your cock truly is exceptional," she exclaimed. "Oh... It feels so good... Devin, I've made up my mind. I won't kill you, and I won't leave either. I want to taste this extraordinary cock every day... Oh, my God... Let it only fuck me..."

Devin Brown's gaze darkened. He continued thrusting into her, positioning her to face him. Instinctively, she held onto his neck and ran her hands through his long hair.

Flower Black, already lost in a haze of pleasure from being fucked, realized how close she was to the man. She turned her head and carelessly kissed his cheek, then moved to his neck, licking and sucking until red and purple marks appeared, creating an ambiguous and sensual scene.

The man, however, felt nothing but the urge to relentlessly pound the woman's delicate and smooth back.

Flower Black discovered that she preferred this supported position. The cock penetrated deep, and she felt at ease. The only regret was that she couldn't see the man's expression; she could only feel the powerful thrusts of his waist, driving the hot and thick shaft to repeatedly pound her pussy, creating waves of desire.

Every time she felt the man's grip relax slightly, and wanted to create some distance between them, she was firmly pressed down and continued to be fucked. After a few rounds of this, she grew annoyed and buried her head, biting down on the man's shoulder, leaving a distinct bite mark.

The man felt the pain, his muscles tensing for a second. But then his lower body attacked her pussy even more violently. And it was Flower Black who couldn't endure it anymore.

"Oh... I'm sorry... I won't bite you anymore, slow down... Oh... my God..."

"Smack... Splatter... Splatter..."

"Slurp..."

The only response to Flower Black was the sound of intense fucking reverberating through the bedroom. She felt like this man was going to fuck her dry. Who was the real demon, her or him?

Chapter 29

As she said, in the end, Flower Black became completely infatuated with Devin Brown's body and settled in his house. Ever since that day when they fucked, the man seemed to drop his facade in front of her. He no longer pretended to be carefree and had a nasty temperament that made Flower Black consider killing him multiple times. However, she couldn't bear to actually do it.

Time passed, and the two of them ended up living like an old married couple. Of course, Devin Brown also used her power to accomplish many things and eventually fulfilled his own desires.

Flower Black stayed by his side until Devin Brown grew old. Before he passed away, a hint of regret appeared on his face, no longer youthful like before. He held the hand of the woman who still had the same youthful beauty as when they first met and said, "It's a pity that I couldn't leave you with a child. In the years to come... you will surely feel lonely... all alone..."

He never received a response from Flower Black in the end, and he didn't know that she didn't care.

As Flower Black coldly watched Devin Brown's students take care of his affairs, she gradually disappeared from sight, but there seemed to be an ethereal female voice lingering in the air, saying, "Parting at dusk, meeting again at dawn..."

Flower Black looked up and chuckled, "How about that? I'm not really a bad demon, am I? You humans just like to categorize and judge. Who said demons involved with human lives can't be good demons?"

The interrogation room fell into silence. It seemed like everyone was still immersed in the story she had just narrated, finding it hard to believe that this spider demon could truly develop genuine feelings and accompany a human until old age.

The woman with short hair snorted coldly, "Who knows if what you said is fabricated. Even if it's true, it's because of your selfishness.

You didn't kill him because you fell in love with him. If it were someone else, would you have stayed with them until old age? I'm afraid you would have devoured them long ago, leaving nothing but bones!"

Flower Black found this metaphor interesting and couldn't help but ask curiously, "If you're not selfish, then if your parents were not good people, but loved you deeply, would you still uphold justice and bring them to justice for their crimes?"

As soon as she finished speaking, a silver whip lashed towards her face. She immediately tilted her head, narrowly avoiding the cold whip. Her face exaggerated a shocked expression, and she let out a long breath.

"Phew... You almost scared me to death! My face is quite valuable. It would be such a waste if it had strange, ugly marks!"

The woman with short hair sneered, "If you know it's a waste, then don't talk nonsense. Otherwise, it won't just be your face that's a waste."

Flower Black was genuinely surprised this time. Well, well! You can use fallacious and irrational arguments, but I'm not allowed to change the subject?

She glanced at the others in the room and saw that they had no intention of stopping the woman. She asked, "Aren't you official organizations? Why are you acting more like villains than me?"

If she remembered correctly, with the development of time, the capturing of demons had evolved from grassroots organizations to official organizations. Not much had changed, except that demon capturing could now be done in the daylight and captured demons couldn't be arbitrarily executed.

Upon hearing Flower Black's question, the others hadn't said anything, but the woman with short hair took a few steps forward, smiling proudly like a chicken. She disdainfully looked at Flower Black and scolded, "Mind your own business! Confess your crimes honestly, and maybe you can plead for your life. At most, we'll return you to your original form!"

Seeing the other party's arrogant appearance, Flower Black instantly understood - It seemed like this woman had powerful background connections! How disgusting!

But she didn't want to break ties with them so quickly. Although there wasn't much difference between doing so and tearing their faces apart now, she hadn't finished telling her story yet! So she lowered her gaze, forcing a few tears out, and said, "I'm really not a bad demon. If the previous story I told doesn't prove it, then let me continue with another one."

It was hundreds of years ago. She worked hard to cultivate her skills, gradually becoming more powerful. But she never gave up on doing good deeds. Every time she encountered a scumbag she wanted to kill, she would casually poison them with her spider venom. She didn't even have to witness the outcome, simply leaving after enjoying some food and fun.

Her spider venom was quite potent. Once it came into contact with the human body, it caused death. For men, it had a strange side effect - it would keep their cocks constantly erect. At first glance, it seemed like a good thing that could even help men with erectile dysfunction. But what if the erection wouldn't go away? Staying hard for several days, even if the poison didn't kill him, he would eventually die because of this side effect.

Like this, she wandered through the human world for several rounds, experiencing the changes of dynasties. On one particular day, at a street corner, she saw a young man riding a horse carelessly through the street.

She followed him invisibly and lightly landed on his horse's back. The young man was completely unaware, whipping the horse's hindquarters without any regard for colliding with pedestrians as he sped ahead. He was followed by a group of servant guards.

Sitting on the horse, Flower Black felt that this scene seemed familiar. Wasn't this the wasteful and arrogant behavior that Devin Brown had mentioned, squandering food?

She stared at the back of the young boy's head with complicated eyes, feeling that it was truly... what goes around comes around.

She followed The young man all the way back to his family mansion and could tell that he was greatly favored by his elders. It could be said that he got whatever he desired - fine clothes, luxurious food, silk, jewels - just reach out and they were his.

It seemed like a noble family, where these things were always abundant. As a result, they raised a young man who cared about nothing but eating, drinking, playing, and having fun.

Flower Black crossed her legs and sat on a beam, supporting her cheek as she looked down. She thought it was fine like this. Devin Brown probably hadn't experienced such a life in his early years. Everything he told her about was the story of his efforts and striving. The easily obtainable wealth and luxury didn't exist for him.

She thought that time would gradually make her forget that short period of experience. After all, as one lives for a long time, memory tends to deteriorate. Why would a demon purposely remember such things?

With their long lives, it was best for them to go with the flow and focus on cultivation. However, the spider demon inexplicably remembered the time she lived with that man, Devin Brown - the trivial little things. It seemed that she still had impressions of them. Truly strange...

It was very strange indeed. Despite having the same soul and the same face, their personalities were completely different, and their life experiences were not the same. Familiar people and names were completely different. So, was this person still the same person from before?

Chapter 30

Flower Black had set up a web on the ceiling of his room and prepared to settle here. She observed this young man just as she had observed Devin Brown before.

So she came to know that this young man was named Henry Lee, nineteen years old this year, the eldest son in his family, with two younger brothers, all born to his biological mother. Their relationship was good and the family was happy.

His father was the third younger brother of the emperor and was born into a prince's family. Moreover, it seemed that there was a genuine brotherly affection between his father and the emperor, and his position was very secure.

Although the young man was arrogant and luxurious in nature, despite being the eldest son, showing no hint of maturity. Occasionally, he would lead his friends to engage in cockfighting or go to brothels where he would be surrounded by beautiful women and encouraged to drink. He was a true dandy.

Seeing various expressions on that familiar yet unfamiliar face, Flower Black found it interesting.

And so, Flower Black, invisible, followed him all the time, occasionally tasting the food and wine while he was enjoying liquor in the brothel. The seasons changed, and a year went by in the blink of an eye.

Summer was a season when all living things felt tired. One afternoon, Flower Black, in the form of a spider, was sound asleep on the web. In her half-asleep state, she accidentally turned over and with a thud, fell into the arms of the young man who was also napping at that moment.

Henry Lee was dreaming. In his dream, the corridor was long and twisted. He walked for a while without seeing anyone else, so he chose

106

a comfortable spot to sit down. Suddenly, he felt a pillow in his arms, but it was not very comfortable to hold, with some prickly sensations...

When he woke up, he was still a bit dazed. Without opening his eyes, he instinctively wanted to call someone to serve him. However, before he could speak, he felt a heavy weight on his chest and the sensation in his hand was off. When he opened his eyes, he met the gaze of four round, pitch-black eyes. His eyes darted around until he saw what was crouching on his chest. He almost couldn't catch his breath and his trembling lips were about to call for someone to come and remove the spider...

It's not that he was timid, but this spider was ridiculously huge! Covered in fur! The size of a baby! This thing might just bite off his head!

Seeing how scared he was, Flower Black transformed into a human form with satisfaction. So, the call that the young man was about to make was swallowed back.

Looking at the pillow beside him and the beautiful woman wrapped in a transparent gown, Henry Lee blinked his eyes and, with a dream-like expression, asked, "Who...who are you? Are you a monster?"

Flower Black stared at the young man with interest, like she was looking at her prey. She raised her hand and the hanging curtains fell, trapping the two of them in the bed.

"Yes... As you have seen, I was that big spider just now..."

Confirming his suspicions, The young man's face turned paler. He trembled and asked, "What...what do you want? Are you going to eat me?"

Flower Black covered her mouth and chuckled lightly. As she laughed, her snowy white bosom trembled slightly. She looked at The young man, who was both scared and staring at her breasts, his eyes wide open. Flower Black thought to herself that he was quite different from the previous person she encountered. She revealed a ferocious expression, pretending to threaten him, "Yes, I am here to eat you. I have been following you for a year, seeing you just idling around all day, engaging in meaningless activities. It wouldn't be a pity to be eaten by me!"

Unaware of the true intentions behind Flower Black's words, Henry Lee thought she really wanted to eat him. Tears started to well up in his eyes, and he choked up in front of Flower Black. With a determined face and his chest puffed out, he bravely said, "If you want to eat me, then eat me! Just leave after you're done! Don't eat the rest of my family!"

Moved by Henry Lee's courageous spirit to sacrifice himself to save his family, he didn't notice the mocking look in Flower Black's eyes as she regarded him as a foolish boy. "When did I say I wanted to eat your family? I only want to eat you, no need for any more nonsense. Undress!"

Henry Lee froze, realizing that no matter what, the other party only wanted to kill him? His choking sounds became louder, but he had no choice but to comply with what she said.

As he started undressing, he felt that something was off... Were demons so particular and troublesome when it came to eating people? Did he really have to undress before being eaten?

Wait... Something doesn't seem right with these words! They sounded like the flirtatious words exchanged between guests and courtesans in a brothel...

He secretly glanced at Flower Black, unsure if his shy and cautious appearance, clutching his collar, resembled that of a young girl experiencing her first time.

Flower Black rolled her eyes, clearly aware that he was not an innocent virgin anymore. When she first encountered him, his family had already arranged for a maid to satisfy his carnal desires. How did it seem like she was forcing the pure-hearted boy...

She sat up, and the collar of her shoulder slipped down to her arm, revealing most of her breast. However, she paid no attention to it and instead reached out to help the (supposedly) innocent boy on the other side quickly remove his clothes.

Henry Lee, witnessing the bold behavior of this spider demon, didn't know whether to cover his manhood or to shift his gaze away from her breasts he had been staring at.

Wow... They're so big, both breasts are large and perky. He had encountered a milkmaid in his friend's estate before, who was specially trained for his pleasure. He even took a sip, but didn't like the taste and never tried it again. That milkmaid's breasts were already quite large, but compared to the spider demon in front of him, they were even bigger, white and perky. It made him unable to resist the urge to pounce and grab them.

If Flower Black knew what he was thinking, she would definitely give him a slap on the forehead, knocking his silly thoughts out of his head.

Comparing himself to someone of her status and even wanting to pounce and grab her, did he think he was a dog?

She might not be a real person, but he was indeed a real dog!

However, Flower Black, despite her profound cultivation, didn't possess mind-reading abilities. Therefore, Henry Lee narrowly escaped a disaster.

He pitifully covered his gradually swelling manhood, completely stripped by Flower Black, occasionally choking and feeling extremely anxious.

Flower Black looked at the somewhat fragile physique of the young man in front of her and doubted if he had reached his full potential. But she couldn't help but feel that if she didn't give him some stimulation, he might remain like this after a few more years, with no muscles on his body. How would that give her any pleasure?

Impatiently, she brushed away the young man's hand covering his lower body and pushed him down onto the bed.

Earlier, perhaps she didn't have a good grasp of force, coupled with his instinctive dodge, Flower Black felt like she had slapped the young man on his already erect manhood. She could hear the young man suddenly gasp, clearly feeling uncomfortable, and then he lay down on the bed even more disheartened.

Chapter 31

Flower Black knelt on the bed, her eyes lowered as she looked at the naked young man. His cheeks were slightly flushed, his body fair and slender. Due to lack of exercise, he didn't have much muscle on his body, but underneath him, his manhood stood tall towards his panties.

He already knew the kind of "eating" that Flower Black mentioned. There was a tinge of anticipation in his heart, but also some unease. Although this woman was beautiful in a way he had never seen before, she was still a demon. He had witnessed her transform from a gigantic spider into a captivating woman. The thought of engaging with such a terrifying spider made him panic.

However, he was used to comforting himself. His pampered upbringing meant he hadn't experienced much hardship, so he was actually quite courageous. Most people would have fainted at the sight of a giant spider crouching on their chest, but he could still have a normal conversation with the demon...

Well, not exactly normal. That teary-eyed, pitiful appearance was quite different from his usual reckless behavior...

Flower Black used a finger to lift Henry Lee's chin, sighing softly with an expression of pity, "Look at this handsome and cute face, I will take good care of you..."

After saying that, she straddled the young man's waist by lifting her leg. Although Henry Lee was young, the cock between his legs resembled a weapon.

Flower Black lifted her hips and rubbed against it with her buttock groove, her voice soft as she asked, "Your body is so slender, without a trace of muscle, why is your cock so big? Did all the nutrients go into growing your manhood?"

Henry Lee's face turned red, and he felt that the woman beneath him was not wearing any clothes. A soft and wetness pressed tightly against his lower abdomen, and the skin that touched him was smooth and tender. Not to mention, the woman had just lifted her hips and rubbed his erect member with her buttock groove. In that instant, a surge of pleasure rushed through his brain like an electric shock, leaving him unable to respond to the woman's words.

Although he had some sexual experience, he was by no means experienced, especially considering the fact that she was a woman of authority, adding a unique excitement to the encounter.

As Flower Black rubbed against the young man's body with her mound, she used her hand to stroke the member behind her. Perhaps finding this position inconvenient, she straddled her beautiful leg and adjusted herself, leaning over between the young man's legs. With both hands holding her large breasts, she sandwiched his member between them. Her dripping wet pussy was right at the young man's mouth. Whenever he lowered his head, he could touch the soaked lips with his lips, which were drenched in lustful fluids.

Feeling his cock wrapped in soft and smooth skin, occasionally squeezed and stroked, he couldn't help but moan, "Oh... My cock feels so good, big sister... Your breasts are so big and tight!"

Warm breath escaped and sprayed onto Flower Black's pussy. As a result, Henry Lee moaned a few times and saw a slow flow of liquid with a floral scent seep slowly from the crevice in front of him. It not only stained the surroundings with a glistening shine but it was evident that there was so much that her pussy couldn't contain it all, and it was about to flow onto his neck.

He didn't pay too much attention to it at the moment. Subconsciously, he lowered his head and sucked up the drops of liquid that hadn't fully dripped, into his mouth. He felt as if his taste buds were overwhelmed with the aroma of flowers, as if he had just consumed pure flower nectar, leaving him with an endless aftertaste.

He saw the woman's buttock twitch twice, and just as he was about to continue licking upwards, he realized that the tip of his tightly gripped member suddenly became hot. It felt as if he had entered a warm and moist place. With the tongue of the woman teasing him, he realized that she was using her mouth to pleasure his big cock. His mind swirled, and he lowered his head to completely devour the woman's pussy.

Flower Black let out a whimper. Her voice was somewhat muffled due to having the cock in her mouth.

Perhaps the young man had never licked a pussy before, so the first time felt very unfamiliar. However, despite never having experienced it personally, he had heard many stories about it. Some people emphasized the delicacy of the experience, while others spoke of more vulgar acts. In the past, he didn't think anyone was worthy of allowing him to do such a thing, especially not the maids who often served him meat. But this enchanting older woman made him give up his virginity, and he didn't feel unwilling in his heart, which was strange.

Flower Black had no idea that the young man could think so much about eating pussy. She only felt his cock making her mouth sour as his tongue became more and more agile, licking her folds until they trembled.

The young man didn't have the self-awareness that he was pleasuring a spider demon with his mouth. He held the woman's big ass in his hands, spreading it open and burying his face in her pussy. He enjoyed it, occasionally pushing his tongue inside and extracting sweet juices with a couple of thrusts, drinking it up.

"Sister, your pussy smells so good... I'm enjoying it so much; I want more of your nectar... Oh..."

Hearing the young man's vulgar and lascivious words, Flower Black's heart stirred. She then used her tongue to rub against his glans, causing him to jerk suddenly. His whole body tensed up, and he ejaculated onto her tongue.

Flower Black frowned unhappily when she unexpectedly had his thick cum filling her mouth. But she swallowed it down and turned her head to look at Henry Lee dissatisfied. However, she noticed that the young man's eyes were already filled with tears, seemingly unable to believe how short his stamina was. He explained with a touch of grievance, "I'm not usually like this. Let's try again, shall we? I promise to satisfy you, good sister. Will that be okay?"

Flower Black remained expressionless, but when she saw that Henry Lee's cock hadn't gone soft even after ejaculating, she couldn't help but marvel at his youthful vigor. Thinking about how, in his previous life, he could still perform on her despite his old age, she naturally didn't hold any grudges against Henry Lee for their short first time together.

However, the young man saw this as a humiliation. He sat up and, in an unprecedented assertive move, pushed Flower Black down onto the bed, eager to prove his ability right away.

Flower Black didn't have to move to enjoy, so naturally she didn't resist. Instead, she obediently lay down. The position she lay in presented her mature and voluptuous body to the young man's eyes, causing him to slow down his rhythm. The two long-awaited big breasts were right in front of him, just as he had imagined before in his mind. He eagerly reached out and grabbed the breasts, bringing them to his mouth to suck on.

The red nipples stood erect on the smooth breasts, blossoming as he licked and sucked on them. He only felt the sweet and delicious taste of the flesh in his mouth. These were the most delicious breasts he had ever tasted. He wanted to wake up every day and bury his head in between these breasts, ravishing them to his heart's content, staining them with his own color and scent.

He went from sucking on them greedily to teasing them sensually. Flower Black stroked his head, her face displaying pleasure and restraint. She let out a few moans through her bitten lips, "You have got hold of sis's nipples... Oh... You're licking me so good..."

Chapter 32

Henry Lee lifted one of the woman's legs and gasped, saying, "Good sis, I'm going to fuck you now. My big cock will be inside your pussy soon. Sis, you have to squeeze it tightly..."

As soon as he finished speaking, Henry Lee supported his cock and thrust into the wet hole that was filled with juice. Flower Black, who was already prepared, didn't feel uncomfortable at all. She only felt a big and long cock enter her without any pause, filling her up completely. The hardness of the young man's member made one marvel at his youthful vigor.

He wrapped Flower Black's legs around his waist, gripping her waist as he thrust and fucked. One of his hands would occasionally squeeze the heaving big breasts that were bouncing with each thrust. When he was completely satisfied, he couldn't help but lean down and kiss Flower Black's tight lips, his tongue parting her lips and teeth, ravaging her mouth recklessly. At this moment, he seemed to revert back to his domineering manner, not allowing the other party to dodge, tightly entwining his tongue with Flower Black's, licking and devouring her mouth.

Flower Black was entwined to the point of impatience, wanting to push him away with a slap. However, with his cock thrusting in and out, sometimes speeding up and fucking vigorously, and his hand twisting her sensitive nipples, she couldn't separate her mind from the intense pleasure. She had no choice but to go along with him.

Feeling that he had thoroughly tasted the woman beneath him, the young man released her lips, but changed his position to a squat. He held the woman's legs in his hands, pulled her closer, and thrust his waist forward with force. His cock immediately pounded deep into the deepest part of her hole. Seeing the woman getting fucked until her toes curled and hearing her continuous moans, the young man maintained this position and went on a frenzied rampage with his lower body.

The woman's hole was originally top-notch, with nine bends inside, tight and enticing, soft and wet, filled with sweet fluid. Henry Lee's cock penetrating and pulling out each time was a test of his willpower. He felt as if there were countless mouths sucking and massaging his cock, making him desire to continue but also to release, unable to stop.

Sweat gradually dripped down his forehead, in the bedroom, the only sounds heard were the gasps and moans of the young man and the woman, as well as the sound of the pounding of the hole.

"Oh...... God boy, your big cock is fucking me to death..."

Seeing the woman's satisfied look after being fucked, the young man couldn't help but feel smug. Sometimes, he and his friends would go too far and have competitions using their cocks. They would choose a few clean maidservants, one each, to see whose cock was bigger, whose stamina lasted longer, and whose technique could make the maidservant climax in the shortest time.

Although he had only played three times, his cock was widely recognized as big and long-lasting. One time, he even made the maidservant squirt, and after that, whenever she saw him, she couldn't wait to suck and clamp his cock in her hole.

However, he wasn't really enthusiastic about this. His family was also afraid that he would be led astray if he did it too much, so they just let him taste it and warned him not to get addicted.

In general, most of the time, Henry Lee listened to his family's advice. Even if there were such activities later on, he rarely fucked with his cock. At most, he let others suck it, but the duration was usually exceptionally long.

The fact that he was sucked by a woman in a short time just now was unforgivable to him. Even if she was a demon, he had to prove the ability of his cock!

Flower Black, who was being vigorously fucked by the big cock, had no idea about Henry Lee's thoughts. She only felt that this cock seemed different from the one in her previous life. When it ground deep inside her, besides the surging pleasure, it also gave her a sense of stealing pleasure.

Chapter 33

"Oh... don't go in any further... It's poking to the end... Oh... Oh, my God..."

Under Henry Lee's vigorous thrusts, Flower Black couldn't hold on any longer. Soft and tender moans escaped her lips, and her hands had nothing to grab onto. The silk sheets were too slippery, making it difficult for her to hold on. She could only fumble around haphazardly, only to have her hands held down by the young man closer to her the next moment.

He re-positioned the woman's legs around his waist, holding down her restless hands that wanted to break free. The hot and rigid cock showed no mercy and continued its assault. Under the continuous physical collision, the ground beneath them became muddy.

Flower Black, who was fucked into a daze, wanted to take back her previous thoughts. She decided not to urge the young man to exercise and build muscles anymore. Even with his small stature, he was able to fuck her for so long. If he were to exercise a little, she might be the one who ends up at a disadvantage.

Not knowing how much time had passed, or how many orgasms she had experienced, when the soft sound of a maidservant knocking on the door came from outside, Henry Lee knew it was almost time. He suddenly accelerated the pace of his thrusts and released himself inside the woman's hole, letting out several sexy gasps.

He saw that the woman had been fucked into a limp state. When his cock was pulled out, she instinctively rubbed against the pillow she had been resting on, her lower body still tightly suctioning him, as if trying to hold on to him. He couldn't help but smile, unable to see any trace of his earlier stuttering and stammering.

The maidservant outside the door called out "Young Master" cautiously twice, but received no response. Instead, she heard some strange noises, making her face filled with suspicion.

Henry Lee had several personal maids, and this one happened to be the one he had fucked before, named Lucy. She often flaunted herself in front of the other maidservants, taking pride in her intimate relationship with the young master. She had always believed that Henry Lee treated her differently from others and had already considered herself as his future concubine.

She was initially sent by the Madam to call the young master over, but as she listened to the commotion inside the room, she felt that something was off. It sounded like she could hear a woman's voice.

She became suspicious and approached the door, pressing her ear against it to listen carefully.

Henry Lee was tidying up his clothes. He didn't ask the maid outside to come in and serve him. After he finished dressing, he bent down and pressed his cheek against Flower Black's face, then turned his head to lightly kiss her ear, playfully saying in a sweet voice, "Good sister, what's your name? Can you tell your little brother?"

Flower Black didn't move at all. She glanced at him blankly, not answering his question. She just turned over and faced away from him, disdainfully saying, "If you don't leave soon, that little maid of yours outside the door won't be able to resist pushing the door open."

Henry Lee's face darkened. He turned his head to look at the tightly closed door, intending to playfully plead with the woman on the bed. However, when he looked back, there was no one on the bed... At the moment he turned his head, she disappeared...

He paused for a moment, realizing once again that the one he had just been intimate with was not a normal person, but a demon.

The door was about to be opened when Lucy caught a whiff of a familiar scent - the scent left behind after the union of a man and a woman. She felt a jolt in her heart and instinctively wanted to peek into the room to see which woman had managed to seduce the young master in broad daylight. She had even started to plan how to report this to the Madam, consumed by jealousy. She was completely oblivious to the uneasy expression on her young master's face upon seeing her.

Henry Lee was in a good mood originally, but before he could even inquire about the demon sister's name, he was interrupted. He couldn't help but find this maidservant increasingly displeasing.

"What is it?" he asked with a cold face.

Lucy finally regained her senses, and quickly bowed to Henry Lee and said, "Madam has ordered this servant to call for you, as if the young master from your hometown has arrived, bringing many gifts."

Upon hearing the title of the young master from his hometown, Henry Lee immediately pictured a face he hadn't seen in a long time in his mind. The restlessness in his heart instantly subsided. He turned and closed the door behind him, taking large strides towards the main hall in the front courtyard, leaving the maidservant far behind.

Lucy bit her lip and tugged at her handkerchief. It felt like ants were gnawing at her heart. She still hadn't seen which shameless woman had seduced the young master! Or...

She looked around, but there was no one else around. So, she quietly pushed open the door that Henry Lee had just closed. She confirmed that she had indeed heard a woman's voice earlier, and only the young master had come out. If there really was someone else, they must still be inside the room.

After searching the entire room, she couldn't find the woman who should logically be there.

With a confused expression on her face, she sat by the bed and saw that it was indeed in disarray, with many ambiguous stains on it, but there was no sign of a person... She sat down and thought for a moment, her face gradually turning red... Could it be... she had misheard and the young master hadn't slept with another woman, but had just pleased himself after waking up from a nap?

As soon as she thought of this possibility, all the discomfort in her heart disappeared, and instead, she thought of her master's remarkably endowed member, feeling a warmth in her heart. She also remembered the only time she had an intimate encounter with the young master.

It was one year ago, in a summer. The weather was hot, and several young masters didn't want to go out but still wanted to have fun. So, they arranged to come to the Wei Residence and participated in that lascivious competition...

At that time, the young master had a lazy expression and lazily pointed at her.

It was her first time gripping the young master's enormous cock without any barriers. Just looking at it was enough to make one lose control. She had fantasized about it many times, but when she took it into her mouth and the young master flipped her over on the bed, spread her legs open, and forcefully fucked her, she realized that all her fantasies couldn't compare to the real sensation.

In the end, she finally squirted while being fucked by the young master. She still remembers how pleasurable it felt, how loudly she screamed. When the young master pulled out, she crawled over eagerly and let him come on her face. The taste of his cum, she couldn't forget for a long time. Just seeing the young master made her weak in the knees, with his perfect face and the wild and unrestrained expression when fucking her.

Flower Black lay on the beam, her beautiful legs hanging on the cobweb she had spun, swaying slightly. Her seductive eyes were full of interest as she watched the maid sitting on the side of the bed and unbuttoning her clothes to touch herself. She clicked her tongue in amazement.

These servants nowadays are really something. They dare to barge into their master's bedroom and even sit on the master's bed to masturbate. As she admired the maid pleasuring herself, she couldn't help but think that there must be some unspeakable stories between this little maid and the young master. She suddenly remembered something interesting and eagerly searched in her spider silk bag...

Oh! Found it...

Seeing the pure white flawless bead in her hand, she squinted her eyes and smiled mischievously...

Chapter 34

This was obtained by her in the hand of a extraordinary person one year ago, a Leave Shadow Bead that could record the current image. Unfortunately, this thing is disposable, and the bead is useless when using magic to play back the image.

Fortunately, she bought many of them from that person at the time, but later it seemed that he said he wanted to go to other planes to have a look, and she never saw him again. Also, because she bought many, it didn't matter if she wasted one or two.

After arranging the Leave Shadow Bead, she elegantly lay back, and the soft but tough spider web accurately caught her. After lying down, she gently rubbed against the silk thread, closed her eyes, and prepared to continue dozing off.

Hmm...the summer makes she feel drowsy, but with the mosquito-like moans of the maidservant today, it feels more lively than usual...

After chatting with his cousin for a while, Henry Lee's mother insisted on inviting them for dinner, and only after they were full did they return to their room.

At this time, it was already late, and the maidservant walked ahead, holding a lantern in her hand. She complained about the lazy Lucy who was nowhere to be found, but she felt joyous about being able to spend this part of the journey alone with the young master. She had a hidden hope in her heart. She often heard Lucy claiming to be the love of the young master, knowing that they all had thoughts about him.

The young master was so handsome and young. If they could be his lover, even if only as a concubine, it would be like soaring to the treetops for these servant girls. Who wouldn't want that?

Henry Lee didn't know what the guiding maidservant was thinking, and even if he did, he wouldn't care. There were so many people who wanted to climb into his bed. Could he guess the intentions of every one of them?

He felt a bit inexplicably annoyed. The joy of talking and laughing with his cousin had disappeared. He was somewhat worried that Spider Demon sister had already left his house. He didn't even know her name, and he didn't have the chance to spend more time with her.

He didn't know why, but when he first saw her, he was a little scared. But the more he looked at her, the more he liked her. After the two of them had sex, that last trace of fear towards the strange disappeared completely.

Thinking that she might leave after eating, he couldn't help but quicken his pace and urge the maidservant with the lantern to walk faster.

The maidservant was bewildered by the hasty tone of the young master. Why does he...seem so anxious?

Flower Black had already had enough sleep. When she woke up and found that it was dark outside, she didn't move from her spot. She just lifted her leg and turned slightly, propping herself up to glance down. There was no one else in the room, but she noticed that the Leave Shadow Bead was still hanging in the corner, being pulled by the spider silk. A satisfied smile appeared at the corner of her mouth.

Not long after, when she felt the drowsiness creeping back, the door of the room opened. Henry Lee, with a hint of alcohol on him, walked in and forcefully slammed the door shut, leaving the maidservant who was going to serve him outside.

Ignoring the maid's resentful expression, he looked around the room as soon as he entered, almost searching every corner. After realizing that there was no one else present, he slumped down on the edge of the bed, his expression resembling that of a lost puppy when its owner runs away, looking adorable in his desolation.

Flower Black lay on the spider web, lazily swinging her legs, coldly watching The young man's frantic search and admiring the expression of disappointment when he couldn't find her. When he sat on the edge of the bed, feeling frustrated, she withdrew her illusion. The young man immediately felt something above his head and abruptly looked up, meeting a pair of slender and enchanting eyes.

The young man was shocked by the massive spider web above his head. In this moment, he didn't fear his room becoming a spider's nest, but instead, he was captivated by the woman's seductive posture. Her fair and slender legs casually draped over the black spider web, her black hair cascading over her barely covered chest. Her partially concealed and mysterious body intertwined with the symbol of darkness, appearing both gorgeous and giving him a thrilling sensation. She had a slight smile on her lips and a teasing look in her eyes, as if mocking his helplessness.

But he couldn't help himself. He believed that no one could react better than him when faced with such a beautiful scene. The moment he saw the woman, his manhood became aroused. No one had ever made him feel this way before. He even felt that even if she had malicious intentions, like a demonic being from a folk tale, wanting to drain his vitality and kill him, he couldn't summon any disgust or rejection in his heart.

He only wanted to possess her, to penetrate her with his manhood, so that she could no longer easily display such a seductive posture to tempt him and make him look foolish.

However, the demonic being was so unattainable. He knew that if she wasn't pleased, she could silently leave at any time, and then he would never be able to find her again. So, he had to temporarily suppress all his dark thoughts and put on a helpless and harmless appearance, silently pleading, "Good sis, baby brother has been thinking about you all afternoon, it hurts so much. Please come down and love me, okay?"

Chapter 35

His voice was soft and husky. The young man didn't know that no matter how he pretended to be weak and vulnerable, his body had already betrayed him.

A pitiful boy with an erection straining against his clothes, raising his erect cock and saying, "Come and love me," sounded more like he was saying, "Come down and let me fuck you to death."

Flower Black couldn't help but let a smile play on her lips. She lifted her arm lightly and floated down from the top. The young man's face brightened when he saw that the woman had indeed come down from the ceiling. He rushed forward to greet her but was surprised when something was suddenly thrust into his arms.

A round and translucent glass bead?

Henry Lee puzzledly examined the bead in front of him. He thought this was a gift from Flower Black, and was about to thank her with a smile when the bead suddenly underwent a transformation.

The surface of the crystal-clear bead seemed to be enveloped in a layer of grayish-white mist. As the mist dispersed, he widened his eyes and exclaimed, "Lucy?"

Not giving him a chance to make random guesses, Flower Black approached him and tapped the Leave Shadow Bead with her fingertip. She said, "This is what she did in your room this afternoon. I just reproduced it for you to enjoy with me. Well, what? Did you think I imprisoned her in the bead?"

Henry Lee knew that his expression just now probably looked like he suspected that she had done something bad. But in reality, he had just never seen such a rare object before. He wasn't afraid that she would harm him.

Not knowing how to explain his thoughts, he carefully held the bead and looked at Flower Black's expression. He realized that she didn't seem displeased, so he shifted his gaze back to the bead.

But when he saw what the other person was doing, his face darkened.

How dare this maid touch herself on his bed!

Seeing that maid's hand reach under her skirt, causing it to float along with her movements, and her flushed face and moans calling out for him to fuck her and ravage her slutty cunt, Henry Lee felt like the bead in his hand was heating up, making him want to immediately throw it away. But because it belonged to Flower Black, he was afraid of angering her if he threw it away.

But he was even more afraid that she would find out about some of the shitty things he had done in the past, disgusted with his unclean cock and his promiscuity. So he discreetly tossed the bead far away onto the bed, pretending not to see it, and innocently said to Flower Black, "Good sis, this servant is too audacious. She dared to do such things in my room! I'll sell her as soon as possible!"

Flower Black had originally had her arms around his neck, rubbing her cheek against his as they embraced. But upon hearing his nonsense, she straightened up and moved away.

Looking at the young man's anxious and uneasy appearance, she thought to herself that he was indeed the same stinky man from their past life, uttering not a single truthful word.

Seeing Flower Black's expressionless face, Henry Lee grew panicked. In a moment of impulse, he took off his pants right in front of her, lifted his shirt slightly, revealing his dripping cock, with two full testicles hanging below. His eyes glistened with moisture as he gently waved his erect cock in his hand, swaying it back and forth.

"Good sis, I'm sorry. Please punish me. Punish this disobedient cock of mine. I promise to only fuck you, sis. All those things I did before I met you were just nonsense. From now on, this cock belongs to you alone."

Flower Black approached and grasped his cock, slowly stroking it. She teasingly said, "Punishment? I'm not so sure about that. Look how excited you are, you're even leaking. Do you secretly hope to be spanked or have your glans pinched by me?"

As she spoke, Flower Black bent her finger and lightly flicked the young man's thick and hard shaft, causing him to softly gasp and pant in her ear. Unable to control himself, he extended his tongue and tasted Flower Black's earlobe.

"Oh... Good sis, flick it again, or even use your palm to slap me. I've done wrong and I want to be punished by you, whether it's slapping my cock or something else, I can accept it. Oh... My cock is so hard, it's incredibly hard. Sis, please touch it..."

Flower Black was aroused by the young man's seductive appearance, her private parts drenched. Though she wanted to push him down right there and sit on him, seeing how much he longed to be punished, she couldn't bear to not satisfy him.

So she pushed Henry Lee away and commanded him to lie on the bed.

Henry Lee reluctantly moved onto the bed, eager to lie down and spread his legs wide open. Even though his cock was already rock hard, he resisted the urge to touch himself and instead eagerly watched the woman who joined him on the bed.

Flower Black pretended to be angry and coldly said, "At such a young age, being so promiscuous. It seems like I need to teach you a lesson."

After saying those harsh words, Flower Black leaned down and took the hard and throbbing shaft into her mouth. She gave a few quick strokes before slapping it once, controlling the force to give him a mix of pain and pleasure. Under this combination of pain and pleasure, Henry Lee's cock quickly twitched, ready to release, but Flower Black quickly wrapped a strand of silk around the base, preventing the impending eruption of semen.

Henry Lee's face was covered in sweat, his brows tightly furrowed. He kept begging, "Good sis, spare me! I know I was wrong. Sis, you're so amazing. Let me release, please!"

As Flower Black slid her fingers along his cock, she softly asked, "Are you still horny?"

The young man looked at her with pleading eyes and replied, "I'll only be horny for you from now on. Let me release for sis, please... Can I climax for sis? Is that okay?"

Amidst his constant whining, Flower Black untied the silk and enjoyed watching as the young man's vigorous member shot out its milky liquid. Even if he accidentally shot some onto her face, she didn't mind.

Since she had fulfilled his desires, it was now her turn to take the lead.

Flower Black didn't pay attention to the liquid still hanging on his glans. She straddled him and sat down, despite the fact that his cock had just experienced an orgasm and hadn't softened. As soon as the hard and throbbing shaft entered the silky and wet passage, it was enveloped by the surrounding tender flesh, instinctively driving him to thrust his hips faster and penetrate this exquisite female body.

Flower Black sat down fully once again, feeling as if there was a breath trapped in her throat that she couldn't release. Before she could even adjust, the impatient young man grabbed her waist and thrust his hips upwards.

With each deep thrust hitting her core, Flower Black's juices splashed and she moaned, saying, "Oh... naughty little brother, you're so good at fucking. How many women have you fucked with this big cock, tell me... Oh... it feels so good."

Henry Lee realized it was not the right time for such a conversation and decided to lift her up and switch to a kneeling position. Without a word, he entered her from behind, pounding his shaft forcefully, aiming to eliminate any thoughts in her mind with pleasure.

The large shaft thrust in and out of her pussy, following its master's desire, crushing Spider Demon's insides until they became soft. Her sensitive spots were repeatedly assaulted, and eventually, she couldn't bear it anymore and tried to climb forward to escape the cock. But the young man held her waist firmly and dragged her back, thrusting even deeper and harder with his cock.

Finally, after being deeply penetrated over a dozen times, Flower Black screamed and her pussy clenched tightly, releasing a powerful surge of liquid onto Henry Lee's shaft.

Henry Lee felt a slight movement within himself and slowly pulled out his cock. He held her ass in his hands, bent down, and observed closely. As expected, clear and bright fluids flowed from her pussy. He licked his dry lips, knowing that he had made his good sister squirt. Immediately, his lips closed around her sensitive area, his tongue exploring inside, savoring every drop of the sweet nectar, refusing to waste a single drop.

After indulging in the honey, he held his still unfulfilled cock in his hand and once again inserted it into her pussy. His expression showed a complete sense of satisfaction. Ignoring the fact that she had just squirted, he forcefully brandished his large erection, thrusting in and out of her pussy, relishing every sensation. In this moment, his demeanor resembled a man from centuries ago with deep, dark desire in his eyes. Unfortunately, Flower Black had her back turned and couldn't see it.

Chapter 36

Afterwards, Henry Lee intended to keep his word and send Lucy away, but Flower Black stopped him. She playfully touched the young man's smooth face and said, "No need to dismiss her. If you two can get along, it will be because you can't restrain your desires. When that happens, I can help you relieve them. Why make things difficult for a mere maid? Besides...seeing but not being able to touch...isn't that amusing?"

Henry Lee's body trembled after being touched by her, not out of fear, but excitement. He believed that this spider demon must possess some kind of enchanting spell, otherwise, how could he be so infatuated with her? He didn't even feel afraid when she mentioned removing his "third leg."

At this point, he already knew her name was Flower Black, and they had been fooling around for a few days without any signs of abstinence. The young man was full of vitality, readily uniting with Flower Black wherever they pleased, leaving traces of their passion on the bed, the lounge chair, behind the screen, and even in the bathtub.

The maid who was tidying the room blushed with embarrassment when she saw these traces, but not knowing the truth, she mistakenly blamed Lucy. Perhaps it was a misunderstanding or jealousy. Lucy secretly reported to her mistress, saying that an immodest woman was seducing the young master every day.

As for Henry Lee's mother, she was also a clever woman who doted on her son. While she indulged him, she also understood her son well. Although he seemed arrogant on ordinary days, he would never do anything that would truly harm himself or his family. Therefore, she directly called Henry Lee over to personally inquire about the situation.

The answer she received surprised her. Her son, who was always reluctant to discuss marriage, now voluntarily expressed his desire to wed. Furthermore, the woman engaging in dalliances with Henry Lee, as reported by Lucy, turned out to be the daughter of the current Grand Minister. She found it hard to imagine that such a strict and traditional figure would raise a daughter who would illicitly be involved with her son.

However, if the rumors were true, she felt it was not a big deal. So she agreed to send a matchmaker to the Grand Minister's residence.

Meanwhile, Flower Black herself was being treated as a distinguished guest at the Grand Minister's residence. She wanted to have an ordinary human identity but didn't want to randomly take someone else's place. So she put in some effort to find a descendant of Devin Brown's students, not knowing how many generations had passed. She also put some thought into making the person believe that she had a connection with their ancestor's mentor, even using magic to intimidate them, which eventually made them believe her.

Of course, it could also be fear rather than belief...

But none of this was a big problem because the outcome was always favorable.

So on an auspicious day several months later, she put on her wedding dress, waiting for her little beloved to come and bring her home.

The young master of the Prince family was getting married. Although he was just a wastrel, it was still a significant event, not to mention that the wife was the Grand Minister's daughter. This grand wedding ceremony caused quite a stir for a few days.

However, after marriage, the young couple didn't get along as harmoniously as speculated by the outside world. Everyone had heard of the prestigious title of the groom, known for being conservative and upright. It was expected that his daughter would also be a proper young lady. How could she possibly get along well with someone like Henry Lee, who was known to be extravagant and reckless?

Not only did they get along well, but they also indulged in passionate nights together. The "flute" they played at night was the one under Henry Lee's crotch. The spider demon completely wove her web in his bedroom, though it was Henry Lee who enjoyed it the most. Lucy wasn't taken away by them in the beginning, as Flower Black put it, making her see but not have, which added to the fun.

There was one time when they both knew Lucy was behind the screen but pretended not to know. They indulged in a passionate encounter on the other side of the screen, the sounds so close that it felt like it was right next to Lucy's ears. Before her eyes, she could see the silhouette of the young master's thick member. Unable to bear it any longer, she applied to serve in another courtyard.

Henry Lee wiped Flower Black's tight hole and smeared the honey on his fingers onto the woman's nose, smiling, "Are you happy now?"

Flower Black moved closer, taking his Adam's apple in her mouth and gently licking it, "Who's happy? Without Lucy, how can you use this as an excuse to have your cock punished? Hm?"

Angrily, Henry Lee immediately pinned the woman down on the bed and spread her legs, and began to lick her.

Chapter 37

In the interrogation room, everyone listened in awe as the spider demon's eloquence was simply outstanding!

Who could have expected that with just her oral account, she could tell her story in such vivid detail that it felt like watching a movie? This was like a porn film.

Just by listening to her describe her sexual encounters with the young man Henry Lee and the previous Devin Brown, it aroused the desires of the onlookers. You could tell from the way their erections were all standing up. And the only woman present with short hair, who knows if her panties were wet or not?

Was the woman wet or not?

Of course she was, while Flower Black was narrating her story, she had several moments where she wanted to interrupt. She felt that continuing with this kind of narrative would lead to an awkward situation, and also...

She discreetly glanced at the man leaning against the wall and playing with his phone, deeply worried that he too would fall under the spell of this shameless spider demon. She noticed that the pants of other colleagues around were bulging, forming tents...

Although she was momentarily immersed in the story that was being told, involuntarily envisioning herself as the female protagonist and the man as the male protagonist, imagining scenes of being penetrated by him, as soon as she snapped out of it, she felt extremely embarrassed. She increasingly felt that this demon had to be dealt with.

"Snap!"

Another whip struck in front of Flower Black, but this time it was aimed at her face. She glared at that face with envy and started to find it more and more unpleasant. She wished she could tear it apart right there and then, so she couldn't use that appearance to seduce men anymore.

Flower Black saw the short-haired woman's eyes turn red as she raised the whip to strike again, but this time she didn't dodge it. Instead, she looked at her with a smile as the whip landed on a transparent barrier.

"Pfft."

She couldn't help but laugh out loud, "You can't be serious, Miss. Do you really think that I patiently shared my private stories with you earlier because I was powerless? If it hadn't been for shedding my shell recently, do you think I would have been easily caught by that little guy over there?"

After saying that, she seemed unsatisfied and gave a meaningful nod to the armrest of the chair. Suddenly, she leaned forward, her raven-like hair falling on her knees. Her words hit the other person's heart like a heavy hammer, "Are you curious about why you hate me so much? Well, I just found out that your soul ... and the Lucy in my story are exactly the same...! Oh my god... it's unbelievable..."

As soon as she finished speaking, countless strands of silk surged out from behind her, flooding the entire interrogation room like a torrent. Those who reacted quickly managed to raise a protective shield, but they were unable to launch a counterattack for the time being.

At this moment, the man who had been leaning against the corner without looking up suddenly made a move. It could be seen that he suddenly had a few more talismans in his hand. When they touched the strands of silk, they spontaneously ignited without fire, and intense flames erupted, spreading along the silk threads as if to turn everything in front of them into ashes.

Amidst the raging fire, he saw the woman smirk at him, as if there was something unfathomable mixed within. Before he could make any other move, her figure had gradually faded, just like in her story, disappearing before his eyes.

The mortal world remained as lively and boring as ever.

A black giant spider with eight long legs busily weaved its web in the forest. This was a rare uninhabited area, filled with various poisonous insects and plants. Every day, it was accompanied by the noisy sounds of insects and birds. But for some reason, this giant spider felt particularly serene.

Oh...

She stopped her busy legs and pondered, wondering if it was summer again?

Well... it's always a dull life. Let's just finish weaving the web and take a comfortable nap!

Story Five: Lewd God

Chapter 38

In the year 309 of the Adams calendar, after several major disasters reshaped the world, technology regressed continuously. However, in order to survive and live in this world full of ghosts and monsters, people began to believe in various deities.

Aside from the mainstream deities, many strange gods emerged through human exploration. They wouldn't bring good luck or blessings to humans, but instead would bring disasters and suffering.

Due to the lack of civilization, it was difficult for everyone to differentiate between the legitimate gods and the evil gods, also known as the malevolent gods. They could only cautiously observe the changes around them; if there were more good things than bad things, then it was considered a legitimate god, otherwise it was considered an evil god.

But even this couldn't be considered foolproof, as the evil gods had various characteristics and personalities. Some of them enjoyed playing pranks. Whenever humans invited them into their homes, they would voluntarily give them some benefits, making them believe that they were legitimate gods. Once the followers devoted themselves with utmost piety, the evil gods would slowly devour their lives.

Despite the existence of various evil gods, humans still fervently believed in deities. In a world of despair, they would hold onto even the slightest glimmer of hope. Moreover, everyone felt that they wouldn't be so unfortunate as to encounter an evil god.

Kitty White was one of the many devotees who worshipped idols of gods. She was an orphan who grew up in a refugee camp, often experiencing hunger and occasional fullness. As soon as she had a bit of strength, she would go and do some physical labor.

Despite her slender figure, her body was actually composed of tight muscles. She never deprived herself and would spend any money she had on food and other necessities. For someone like her, who could eat their fill while the whole family didn't go hungry, saving money wasn't of great significance.

Thus, since she started working, she ate better and better. She made up for the lack of nutrition from before and now had honey-colored skin, a healthy and well-proportioned body, and a lively smile on her youthful face.

"This is today's wages, take it."

"Hey! Thank you, Uncle Devin!"

Kitty White stuffed the money she received into her coat pocket without even counting it. She greeted Uncle Devin, her boss, and left with her small tattered bag.

The bag was originally made of white canvas, but due to long-term use and being covered in dust, it looked dirty. However, Kitty White cherished it. She picked it up and patted it, trying to clean off the dust. Unfortunately, the canvas material itself held onto the dust, so as she walked and patted, she not only failed to clean it but made it even dirtier.

She shrugged, pretending not to notice, and slung the bag over her shoulder, getting ready to welcome the first deity in her home.

Not everyone can afford to worship a deity. First of all, you need to have some savings. Poor families who can't even afford to eat, how can they have money to buy incense and offerings for the deity?

Secondly, you must be at least 18 years old, an adult. Only adults can take care of the deity properly. Some rebellious teenagers always go against everyone, not only lacking reverence for the deity but even showing great disrespect. Of course, they don't have the qualifications to worship a deity. In fact, people are afraid to invite such individuals back home as it might bring harm. After all, who says that deities must have a good temper?

Kitty White had long passed the age of 18. In fact, she was already 26 years old this year. However, she was never able to save enough money to worship a deity until now.

For someone like her, who lives day by day, saving money was unheard of. It was only when she noticed the neighboring family's situation improving after worshiping a deity that she finally decided to save money and worship one herself.

But because she always felt that this matter was distant from her, she hadn't carefully studied the differences between various deities. She only vaguely understood that most statues of the God of Fortune looked relatively normal, while statues of evil deities tended to look strange. So she determined to worship the most beautiful deity she could find.

There are several temples in every city where deities are worshipped. It was already late when Kitty White finished work, so she took a bus to the city center before it got dark.

As she boarded the bus, she noticed that there were some empty seats, but many people were standing instead, holding onto the overhead rings and either looking out the window or engaging in conversations. Kitty White found a ring without anyone holding onto it and overheard a conversation. One person said, "It's getting hotter these days. I wonder if it will rain tomorrow..." Another replied, "Yeah, the wait for the bus to the city center is quite long. I've been standing here for more than half an hour!"

It was a boring topic, but they seemed quite engrossed in their conversation.

Kitty White didn't want to join in their boring discussion, so she shifted her gaze to the scenery passing by outside the window. As for the empty seats, she naturally didn't think of sitting in them.

In this world where spirits and ghosts roam, everyone tries to avoid doing seemingly ordinary things that actually entail danger, such as empty seats on a bus. Who knows if they are truly empty or if there are invisible occupants? The moment she boarded the bus, she had a strange feeling that the seats were already full, and she believed that the others standing felt the same way.

Chapter 39

When the bus reached her stop, Kitty White glanced at her wristwatch. It was exactly 6 o'clock in the evening. She followed the crowd and got off the bus, looking at the various food stalls set up around her. Her stomach seemed to growl.

In this era, there were no city management authorities maintaining order on the roads. Although it was considered the city center, it was only relatively densely populated and had a relatively concentrated commercial area. There were also many wooden structures with canvas signs hanging above, displaying the names of different shops. At first glance, it felt like she had traveled back to the distant ancient times.

She quickly found the temple she wanted to worship. It was a building that didn't look much different from the neighboring shops, except for its roof, which was painted with red paint in a peculiar symbol, indicating its unique identity.

She showed her identity card at the entrance and followed the guidance of the staff in red uniforms to a cabinet filled with various deity statues. The statues covered three walls, densely packed together, making anyone with a hint of trypophobia feel psychologically uncomfortable.

These statues had completely different faces. Even if two statues looked very similar, upon closer observation, one would notice some subtle differences.

Kitty White, with her discerning eyes, reminded herself to choose the most beautiful one to bring back. So she tried her best to compare the statues on all three walls. The more she looked, the more she questioned her existence. Why did it seem like there were barely any normal-looking ones...

There were statues with two heads, eyes on the chin, or in other odd places. There were many with severely disproportionate body proportions. Some were so bizarrely shaped that it was impossible to discern where their faces were. This made Kitty White inwardly doubt if they were all evil deities. However, her rationality told her it couldn't be true. The authorities had statistically confirmed that the proportion of evil deities was at most one percent. It was impossible for all the statues on three walls to be evil deities.

She suppressed her impatience and looked at each statue again, until finally, in the middle somewhere, she spotted a statue with a kind and benevolent face. The statue's exterior material was unknown but appeared as fair as jade. It sat on a stone throne in a cross-legged position, its eyes slightly closed, and a red vertical scar on its forehead. Long hair cascaded down its bare chest, and a gentle curve at the corner of its mouth gave the appearance a particularly soft and harmless touch. If one ignored the two arms behind it, it seemed like a standard depiction of a deity in a painting.

But Kitty White didn't mind this detail. Compared to the other bizarre statues, this one could be considered beautiful, friendly, and kind!

She had made up her mind! It was going to be this deity!

After the staff member noticed that Kitty White had chosen a specific deity statue, he gave her a strange look.

Kitty White, being sensitive, noticed this and thought that there might be something wrong with her selection. She turned her head and carefully examined the statue again, confirming that it was indeed a statue that she really wanted to take home and worship. When she turned back to the staff member, she found that he had already brought a small wooden cabinet with a dark red lacquer finish.

"This is a shrine, where the Priapus usually resides. When you go back, place the shrine in a separate room and offer three incense sticks every morning and evening," he explained.

Kitty White nodded to indicate that she understood. She carefully packed the shrine and the Priapus's statue into the box provided by the temple. With a sense of unease, she walked out of the temple.

By this time, it was close to 9 o'clock in the evening. It had taken her nearly three hours to make her selection!

She hurriedly held onto the box and quickened her pace. The last bus was at 9 o'clock, but luckily the bus stop wasn't too far away. She managed to catch it just in time.

Chapter 40

The bus to the suburbs in the evening was very empty. People in this world were accustomed to going to bed early to avoid the risk of encountering supernatural events. Entertainment options had become scarce, so there wasn't much to do and people naturally went to bed early.

Therefore, it was understandable that there were only a few passengers on the bus.

Kitty White found a seat by the window that didn't give her any bad feelings and sat down. She contemplated what she needed to do next. Besides continuing to work hard to earn a living and support herself, she now had an additional expense for offering incense at home. She hoped that the Priapus would protect her and improve her situation, as well as protect her from encountering any horrors.

Even though she hadn't started the actual worship yet, she had already begun praying in her heart.

In the darkness, the statue, placed inside the box, seemed to move slightly, as if it was vibrating due to the movement of the bus.

Kitty White lived in a residential area in the suburbs, filled with small two-story houses built side by side. Each house was quite spacious, divided into small rooms of about thirty square meters each.

Living here usually meant being from a relatively well-off family. Those who were even poorer could only live in the wooden houses in the poor district. Those houses were self-built, and not to mention that constructing houses required advanced skills, just finding materials in this dangerous world wasn't as easy as it was in peacetime.

Kitty White's room was the fourth one from the inside, counting from the outside. She took out a key and unlocked the door. She noticed that the neighbor next door had piled up a lot of garbage between their two entrances, causing her eyebrows to slightly furrow.

Then, she carefully bent down and opened the garbage bag to take a look. After glancing at what was inside, she resealed it and went inside her own apartment.

She didn't need to pay attention to the neighbor on the right, who seemed to be a young couple. The neighbor on the left, however, was a middle-aged couple with a son who looked about seven or eight years old.

It should be around seven or eight years old, Kitty White thought uncertainly.

She had never had a conversation with them, but occasionally they would exchange friendly smiles. Kitty White had heard the sound of the neighbor helping their son with homework several times.

These houses could be essentially described as having no soundproofing. Any noise from one house, even if it was a little louder, could be heard by everyone in their own homes.

The reason she paid attention to them was because she overheard other neighbors talking about how they had brought in a god for good luck.

"It is said that they managed to invite the true god, called Sita, and it has been very effective. Since they brought the god back, the man's salary has increased a lot, they have even found money a few times, and their son has become much more obedient. Now the whole family is full of happiness every day!"

Hearing about the increase in salary and finding money, Kitty White was intrigued.

On her way back, she had already decided. Her room was very small, she could see the whole room at a glance. But in order to accommodate Priapus, she could manually create a small partition with a curtain.

She was skilled with her hands, and coincidentally, she had an unused piece of floral fabric that a former coworker had given her for making clothes. She used the wire and fabric she had at home to create a small partition. She then nailed the shrine to the wall and placed a wooden table underneath as an altar. On top of the altar, she placed a bowl with a bread that she had stored in a small fridge.

She carefully placed Priapus in the shrine, took out three incense sticks from the box, and lit them. Sincerely, she recited the blessings and closed her eyes, praying for Priapus's protection and good luck in everything.

She almost repeated the prayers she had made in her heart while on the bus again. Finally, she bowed three times before the shrine and placed the incense on top of the bread.

Early the next morning, she went to the supermarket to line up and buy enough food for herself for two days. She also bought incense sticks for the offerings to the god.

The three sticks she used last night were given by the temple, but from now on, she needed to be prepared with her own supply, which could be found in most supermarkets.

When she returned, she saw that the garbage from yesterday had been thrown away and replaced with new bags of garbage. This time, she didn't go up to open the bags, she simply ignored them and went inside her home.

After washing her hands, she worshiped the god, then took a bread and put it in her bag, getting ready to leave for work.

As a worker with hours dependent on the weather, their daily tasks were not always the same. Yesterday, they could have been carrying sacks, and today they could be cleaning a certain street, also known as street sweeping.

She was one of the few who arrived early today, and when Uncle Devin, the foreman, saw her, his eyes narrowed and the wrinkles on his face deepened. He stuffed the bun in his hand into his mouth, then patted Kitty White's shoulder with his greasy hand and said kindly, "Kitty, the job we talked about yesterday had an unexpected surge in workers. But I took a look and there happens to be a job available in the pharmacy, where they need someone to grind medicine. It doesn't require any particular skills, just a large quantity. The pharmacy hires people to grind enough medicine for a month. If you don't mind overtime, the wages are at least this much."

He gestured with his hand, and Kitty White immediately agreed.

She knew about the pharmacy he was referring to. Nowadays, whenever people have a headache or fever, they usually go to medicine practitioner and take medicine. Those who have connections can become suppliers of medicinal herbs, while those who don't can apply through official channels. In any case, medicine is considered very important, so jobs related to medicine often pay well.

She couldn't believe such a good opportunity had come her way! She promised herself that she would work carefully. Otherwise, it would be a waste of Priapus's blessing!

That's right, she believed that the god she worshipped had heard her prayers!

She never expected it to work so quickly, and she covered her chest, which felt warm with excitement.

No wonder her neighbors have been eating well ever since they started worshipping the god. The trash bags are filled with expensive food packaging or bones.

She felt that if things continued this way, she might have the same fortune!

With her hopes for a better future, she went to work with efficiency.

Chapter 41

Kitty White massaged her sore waist and back, feeling that grinding medicine all day was more tiring than carrying heavy bags.

But as soon as she thought about the money she would be able to earn, she didn't consider it a big deal anymore.

By the time she finished work, it was already dark outside. There were still some medicines that needed to be prepared, but she had to go home for now and come back tomorrow.

To get to her house from the pharmacy, she had to walk through two streets. There weren't many streetlights, but she brought a flashlight with her. As long as she didn't intentionally head towards the corners and paid attention to avoid kicking or stepping on anything she shouldn't touch, it was generally safe.

Moreover, now that she had the protection of the deity, she felt even safer.

However, just as she was approaching the last corner before reaching home, she was startled by a sudden figure appearing.

She took a few steps back and then realized that the person blocking her path was someone she knew. After calming down her disheveled breath, she glared at the man in front of her and asked annoyed, "What are you doing here?"

The man, wearing work pants and a black short-sleeved shirt, scratched his short spiky hair and awkwardly revealed a smile. His eyes, however, gleamed as he stared at the rise and fall of her chest, saying, "I want to fuck you."

Here we go again!

This was Kitty White's co-worker and pursuer, Tony Wilson. He was a tall man, about 1.9 meters, with bulging muscles, but he had a handsome face that exuded a sunny charm.

At first, Kitty White found herself slightly intrigued by his pursuit. After all, he had a good physique and looked decent, and she could tell from working together that he was hardworking and diligent. So she reluctantly agreed to sleep with him once. However, she never expected him to be insatiable. She felt like turning her face right then and there, but she couldn't exactly say, "You've fucked me for too long and your cock is too big, it's uncomfortable for me!"

It would sound like she was complimenting him.

Moreover, this man always liked to wear a small flat head and act cute, looking silly and adorable, completely not her type. She liked the kind of man with a strong and gentle personality, so she would often avoid him.

But Kitty White is a practical jerk. She didn't want to date him, but she wouldn't refuse his gifts either. That piece of floral fabric was obtained in this way.

Listening to Tony Wilson's straightforward language and gaze, Kitty White couldn't help but have some feelings, thinking to herself that she hadn't have sex for a long time. His cock was acceptable, and coincidentally, she was in a good mood recently, so she could consider it.

So she glanced at him, remained silent, but clearly indicated to the man that he should follow her. The two entered the door one after another, and Tony Wilson immediately noticed the changes in Kitty White's home, asking, "Did you invite a deity?"

Kitty White threw her bag on the chair, turned her head to wash up, and replied, "Yeah, my Priapus is so powerful! Don't go in there! Be careful not to offend the god!"

Tony Wilson sat on the edge of the bed and glanced at the floral curtain, saying, "I know, actually, I was also considering getting one recently. But where I live is not as stable as yours."

After not hearing a response from her for a long time, the sound of dripping water came instead. He thought for a moment, then immediately took off his clothes and opened the bathroom door, completely naked.

This bathroom was very narrow, only wide enough for one person to squat inside. If standing up, two people would have to be pressed closely together.

So, while Kitty White was applying bubble foam on her body, she was caught off guard by the man's embrace, holding her tightly.

Her back was pressed tightly against the strong man's body, his rough big hands freely wandering on her body, warm breath swirling in her ears, and she instantly got wet.

She felt a hot rod pressed against her waist, about to moan, when the man seemed to squat down a bit, and the cock slapped against her crotch. He flicked his cock with his hand, like a spring, and the cock slapped against her pussy again with a 'pop'.

Kitty White bit her lip. Has this man been trained? How come he's so good at teasing this time!

"Tony Wilson, you go out first, I'll finish washing, then you can come in, it's too small here, we can't do anything."

Kitty White had to speak up. If she didn't stop him, he would just stuff his cock into her pussy right there.

Tony Wilson's response was to lick her neck a few times, then put his hand down and grab his cock, and stuff it into her hole.

Of course, he knew it was tight here, otherwise why would he take off his clothes and come over for what reason?

"It'll open up, I'll make it open..." he whispered to Kitty White's ear.

Ignoring the sudden blush on the woman's earlobe, he found the hole and thrust with force, sending himself inside.

Although she said it couldn't fit, her already wet pussy had no resistance to this hot cock. With each thrust, her legs softened, her hands groped the wall in front of her, and her ass unconsciously lifted up.

"Fuck! Be gentle!"

She hissed, unable to stop the trembling of her body, while the man behind her began to thrust against her waist.

Every thrust hit her entrance and plunged deep inside, after a few rounds, he started deliberately changing angles, trying to find that most comfortable spot for the woman.

"I heard from my friend that women have a pleasure spot inside their bodies. If you find it while fucking, you'll feel really good. Let me try and see if it's true."

He quietly explained to Kitty White and persistently searched for it with his cock, much to Kitty White's annoyance.

"You told your friends that you had sex with me?" she asked.

The man, panting as he thrust, replied, "Yeah, I bragged to them about how tight and tender your pussy is. They envy me and said they wanted to fuck you too, but I refused. If I can't even fuck you properly, how could I share you with others? Their cocks are short anyway, don't even think about it. Just take mine."

Kitty White, "What the fuck! Who the fuck wants it! Are you sick? Why are you telling unrelated people about these things? Oh......fuck!"

It seemed like Tony Wilson finally hit that critical spot. He felt like the glans scraped against a slightly different tender flesh. His scalp tingled from being engulfed by the wet pussy. He exerted force towards that exact spot. Kitty White was being fucked so hard that her mouth was wide open, and her legs were sliding down weakly.

With a strong pull, the man held the woman back, but his cock kept pounding in her pussy like a pile driver.

Without answering the woman's question, the room was filled only with the sounds of their heavy breathing.

Kitty White felt a moment of blankness in her mind. She clenched her teeth and tried not to moan, but she felt that this sexual encounter was unusually long-lasting.

She couldn't pay attention to the man's strong kneading of her breasts. She was thinking, having sex while taking a shower, with water on her body, the sound of slapping asses would surely be heard by the neighbors, right? Sometimes she could hear the sounds of fucking coming from the next room, but she didn't want to be heard by others behind the wall.

It will definitely be heard!

And she seems to have overlooked something...

She, after being fucked hard, felt a bit confused. Sometimes she thought this man's cock was really powerful and wanted to be fucked by him again next time. Other times, she felt like this man was going to fuck her to death, and she relied on him completely.

Suddenly, she remembered that her Priapus was still there. This effective Priapus must have been watching her all this time, watching her pray to him, and watching her being shamelessly fucked by a tall man.

She didn't know why, but she felt a bit panicked and wanted to escape. However, the space was small, and she had no strength left. She could only be passive and grabbed by the man as he fucked her with his cock.

Her slutty and horny pussy had no idea about her owner's intentions. It just kept tightening around the cock, and the man was driven crazy by it. He fucked her forcefully regardless, and finally released inside her tender pussy, which had been soaked with unknown amounts of fluids.

Without the cock blocking the way, both semen and front holel fluids gushed out from the hole that was stretched by fucking, temporarily unable to be restored.

Tony Wilson hugged the woman tightly and grabbed the showerhead, spraying water onto both of them. He kissed Kitty White's face and said, "You've been fucked loose by me."

Chapter 42

That night, Kitty White had a strange dream. First, she dreamt of herself being fucked by Tony Wilson everywhere, even in various locations, including a temple of pleasure.

She dreamt of the staff member who guided her that day, wearing a red uniform, and a group of unfamiliar people standing around, forming a circle to watch them fuck. She felt both fearful and ashamed being watched, and in the end, she lost control and urinated on the person closest to her in front of everyone.

She dreamt that they had been fucking for too long, and her legs couldn't stay closed anymore. She was fucked loose, and she couldn't hold back the semen he ejaculated inside her. As she walked, the semen continued to flow down her thighs. Passersby saw this and reached out to touch her, and someone even unzipped their pants, wanting to force their cock into her mouth.

The second half of the dream was about a handsome man she had never seen before. He led her out of the scene of lust and showed her around his house.

His house was so grand, with golden carvings and servants everywhere. He only wore a black cloth skirt on his lower body, leaving his upper body naked and revealing his attractive chest muscles. His dark hair fell to his waist, and he lazily leaned on a jade chair, one leg raised and resting on the armrest. As for her, as if enchanted, she crawled under his skirt, grabbed his thick sex organ and became infatuated with licking and sucking it.

She served the man sitting on the throne with her lips and tongue, as if she were a specialized maid for such things. She didn't even miss his testicles and anus.

She savored it carefully and obsessively, as if she were enjoying a delicious delicacy in the world.

People in dreams have no logic and don't think, so she easily followed the development of the dream.

That man seemed to regard her as an ordinary servant. After taking her home, he kept dozing off and no longer gave her a glance. However, she became even more infatuated with him.

She competed with the other maids who wanted to get close to him, using her strength to push everyone away, and satisfyingly took the man's sex organ into her mouth once again.

At this moment, the dozing man slightly raised his eyelids. It seemed as if she saw blood-red eyes, but in the blink of an eye, they became distinct black and white eyes. He looked at her with a smiling and compassionate expression, as if a god were looking at a mortal.

Kitty White woke up all of a sudden. She wiped off the sweat on her forehead and felt that the dream she just had was very strange, but couldn't pinpoint what was strange about it. She only felt that it was all Tony Wilson's fault for saying nonsense about fucking her loose yesterday. Otherwise, she wouldn't have had such a bizarre dream.

Normally, dreams shouldn't have any sensation, but she clearly felt the entire process of being fucked, including the absurd feeling of being obsessed with someone else's cock in the latter part of the dream.

The sky was still dark at this time. She looked at the clock and saw that it was only 5 am.

As she tried to shake off the feeling of that dream, she walked in her slippers, preparing to go to the bathroom to wash her face and wake up.

Looking at herself in the mirror, with bloodshot eyes, Kitty White frowned. She had stayed up too late last night, barely had any sleep, and even continued the affair in her dream. She was so tired that she didn't feel like working today...

But thinking about the money she hadn't gotten yet, she splashed a few handfuls of cold water on her face to clear her mind.

Then, taking advantage of the early hour, she cooked herself a bowl of porridge for breakfast. It was rare to have the luxury of enjoying such a careful breakfast, and her restlessness gradually disappeared.

After finishing her breakfast, she lit an incense stick and made three devout bows, repeating her wish three times in her mind. Only then did she contentedly go to work.

Chapter 43

Today was the last day of her job as a pharmacy assistant. As soon as she entered the store, she bumped into a middle-aged woman who was happily carrying a bag of medicine.

The woman staggered, losing her grip on the bag of medicine and dropping it to the ground. Kitty White hurriedly squatted down to pick it up, feeling sorry, and was about to join the woman in picking it up.

But the woman waved her hand and said, "It's okay, it's okay. I was so happy that I wasn't paying attention to the road."

Kitty White found it a bit strange, but since they were strangers, she didn't want to ask too many questions. After a few more apologies, seeing that the woman didn't seem to mind, she walked into the pharmacy.

"Little girl, the medicinal ingredients are all prepared in the back. You smash them there, and you don't need to come in tomorrow. The wages will still go through the foreman, so you go find him to collect it."

The boss only glanced at Kitty White, his expression unchanged.

Kitty White, however, was curious. The woman's happy expression just now made her wonder if it had something to do with the gods. Perhaps it was because she herself had recently prayed to the gods, and now she tended to think about everything in that way.

So out of curiosity, she couldn't help but ask, "Why was that auntie so happy just now? Is something good happening at home?"

The boss looked up at her and sneered, saying, "Yeah, his daughter-in-law is pregnant. She had some health issues before, and she was coming here to get medicine but still couldn't get pregnant. Then she went to pray to the gods a few months ago, and now she's expecting. I say, can't the gods cure infertility? Maybe the daughter-in-law cheated on her husband!"

The boss's tone was full of disdain and skepticism, which made Kitty White uncomfortable. She had a feeling of suffocating that she couldn't explain.

Instinctively, she retorted, "Maybe it's a miracle!"

The boss frowned, and the wrinkles on his face sharpened. He replied, "You little girl, what do you know?"

Sensing that the atmosphere was not right and realizing that she hadn't received her wages yet, Kitty White didn't dare to argue further. She awkwardly tried to make up for it, "Actually, I think it's also possible that the medicine she got from you before started working, and it just happened to coincide with them praying to the gods, making it seem like a miracle rather than the medicine's effect."

The boss seemed appeased by her explanation. He didn't say much anymore but waved his hand for her to go to the back quickly. Kitty White didn't want to say anything more either, afraid that another argument would arise. She hurriedly pulled aside the curtain and went to the back.

In her heart, she still believed that it must be a miracle. This thought grew stronger when she found a sum of 3,000 dollars on her way home from work.

She carried a secret sense of joy, along with her days' wages and the "windfall" she found, back home.

After putting down her bag at home, the first thing she did was cleanse her hands and hold three sticks of incense to pay respects to Priapus. Her heart was filled with unprecedented piety.

"Kind-hearted Priapus, thank you for the generous gifts. May your name be revered by the world, and may your will be my heart's desire. I pray that you keep your devotee away from disaster and grant her good luck. Everything that your devotee possesses belongs to you!"

Kitty White, earnestly praying with her eyes closed, didn't see that the deity sitting cross-legged on the stone platform had opened his narrow eyes at some point. His bloodshot eyes were filled with cracked blood vessels, and a strange curve appeared at the corner of his mouth. He stared fixedly at the woman who was praying sincerely in front of him.

The brown hair hanging in front of his chest, upon closer inspection, seemed to come to life. It twisted and writhed slowly, occasionally raising its tail, transforming into black venomous snakes that maliciously spat venom in the woman's direction.

Clearly, the deity Kitty White had invited back was not the orthodox god she had imagined, but a genuine evil deity. However, Kitty White was unaware of this terrible truth. She was single-mindedly grateful to this deity who had brought her good fortune twice. While feeling delighted about her own experiences, she also greedily desired more.

So she made many unrealistic wishes, thinking that even infertile women could be cured by deities, and perhaps her own deity would kindly fulfill her insignificant desires.

With these hopeful expectations for the future, she entered her dream.

Chapter 44

That night, Kitty White had a beautiful dream. She dreamed that all her wishes to Priapus had come true. She had a boyfriend as handsome as Priapus, with an extraordinary physique and great wealth. She could have whatever she wanted.

Improving her financial situation meant she no longer had to work hard to support herself. Like her next-door neighbor, she could now enjoy a life where she could eat meat every day. Her excellent boyfriend accompanied her, being gentle, considerate, and understanding. And then she had a lovely baby, and the three of them lived happily every day.

When she woke up, she still had a smile on her face. Lying in bed, she reminisced about the dream, feeling that it must be a hint from Priapus.

As her allotted time for staying in bed approached, she quickly flipped over and got up. However, she saw a stranger sitting by her desk, completely unaware of their presence, despite being so close.

So she was scared, and reflexively moved back a little, but the man suddenly spoke, "Kitty , why did you wake up so early? Do you want to rest a little longer? Are you going to work today?"

A gentle and soothing male voice resounded in this tiny house, pleasant and magnetic. When Kitty White heard this male voice, she froze for a moment and couldn't help but exclaim when she saw the person's face, "It's you!!"

Her face was filled with disbelief.

She was too familiar with this man's face. Wasn't this the same face as her perfect boyfriend from the dream she just had?

It was as if a beautiful pantomime had played out in the dream. Unexpectedly, his voice in reality was so appealing!

Kitty White covered her mouth and still found it hard to believe. Eliminating all the possibilities, there was only one answer that could explain this mysterious coincidence: the gift from the gods!

She quickly accepted this miraculous surprise and began to scrutinize the man who sat at the table with a gentle smile.

Then she felt that everything was perfect! It was extremely satisfying, especially considering his almost identical face to Priapus.

Instead of sitting down to enjoy the breakfast prepared by the man, Kitty White took a few steps forward and pulled back the floral curtain. When she saw Priapus still sitting on the stone seat without any movement, she finally relaxed.

Proficiently, she took three sticks of incense from the nearby shelf, lit them, and offered prayers to the deity with a complex mood before turning back to sit at the table.

She picked up the fork but couldn't bring herself to eat the food several times.

The table was filled with delicacies that she rarely had the chance to eat, exquisite breakfast that made her appetite soar, but at a glance, they seemed expensive.

She swallowed her saliva and decided to initiate a conversation first. She carefully glanced at the man and asked, "May I ask, what is your name?"

Instinctively, she used honorific language when talking to this man with the face of Priapus.

However, the man supported his face with a gentle gaze to soothe her. He pushed the dish in front of him towards her side and smiled, saying, "Kitty, you don't need to use honorifics. We're boyfriend and girlfriend, right? Just call me Perry."

Perry...

Kitty White silently repeated the name in her mind before cautiously smiling at the other person. She then picked up the food in front of her and started eating.

It wasn't that she wasn't curious about other things, but she was afraid that if she asked the wrong question, it would be like waking up a dreamer and the whole dream would shatter. Who knows if the bestowed god who woke up would disappear?

She decided to just accept that he had always been her boyfriend!

As for Tony Wilson, whom she had just slept with a couple of days ago, she had already put him out of her mind. If you asked her, at most, he was just a casual sexual partner, definitely not her boyfriend.

She felt anxious for a while but then accepted this suddenly appearing boyfriend with a sense of peace. She even began to feel a sense of happiness from their interactions.

Whether it was his gentleness and good temperament, or the fact that he could understand her thoughts and desires even before she expressed them, this perfect match made Kitty White completely immersed in it.

"Oh, so good! Fuck! Honey, your big dick feels amazing... Oh... Need more, want to be fucked into the uterus..."

Kitty White knelt on the bed, the man held her arm, and his lower body thrust and collided with the woman's voluptuous buttocks.

The crimson shaft was covered in the woman's wetness, and with the man's movements, it tantalizingly appeared and disappeared between Kitty White's thighs. But she couldn't see the abnormal color of the shaft herself, she only felt the terrifying pleasure she hadn't experienced in so many years since losing her virginity.

She couldn't even think about whether her moans were too loud and could be heard by the neighbors through the walls.

This was completely different from the previous time with Tony Wilson. Although Tony Wilson had a big and long member, he always just charged in without any technique. Despite the fact that his shaft, due to its size, would make her scream each time, this feeling was different from the pleasure of someone skilled.

The tip of Perry's shaft seemed to have a slight curve, and with every thrust, it stroked against her sensitive walls, grinding repeatedly. And her walls themselves were hot, so when they wrapped around the entire shaft, it felt as if she was being burned by its temperature. Her heart would feel a tingling sensation, and uncontrollable fluids would surge out.

Perry held onto her wrists with one hand, and the intensity of his thrusts didn't diminish at all. And yet, he had a gentle smile on his face. If there was a mirror in front of Kitty White, she would see a mask-like smile on his face.

"Kitty, your pussy is so soft, so good to fuck. Oh, yeah..."

The man praised softly as he pressed against the woman's back. The speed of their thrusting slowed down, and from behind, all that could be seen was their tightly connected lower bodies and the man's tightened buttocks from occasional forward thrusts, giving off a particularly seductive aura.

This intermittent impact further aroused their desires, especially with the sound of wet slapping that came from their muddy lower bodies. Kitty White wondered just how much fluid it would take to make that sound. Not to mention the man's divine face, as though Priapus himself was fucking her. Kitty White couldn't help but blush.

She grabbed her own nipples, her face flushed with desire. But then, the man suddenly pulled out his crimson shaft, buried his head, and his long tongue swept through her soaking wet hole.

Kitty White, whose little hole was being tantalized by a soft tongue, felt an unusual sense of satisfaction both mentally and physically. The man spread her legs wide open, burying his entire head in her pussy. His mouth enclosed her thick folds, and his handsome face was covered in her juices.

After a while, as if he had had enough, he moved his soft tongue to her tight little back hole, gently licking it up and down. The saliva that couldn't be swallowed dripped onto his tongue, coating the cute folds of her puckered entrance.

Feeling the waves of wet pleasure emanating from her lower body, Kitty White couldn't hold back any longer. Clear fluid gushed out from her pussy, and she let out a long moan, clutching the bedsheets beneath her. But then, she suddenly felt a sharp pain, the terrifying sensation of her back hole being stretched open, and this uncomfortable feeling of invasion only grew stronger. It dawned upon her that the man had stuffed his shaft into her freshly licked back hole.

Kitty White wanted to struggle and crawl away, but to no avail. Naturally, she was firmly but gently restrained.

"Don't... don't do this, Perry... it's uncomfortable for me..."

Her attempt to escape once again failed, and instead, her back hole was pushed deeper by the shaft. Kitty White tried to plead for mercy, but all she heard in response was a faint, ambiguous chuckle.

The man leaned down and licked her cheek, while at the same time, he forcefully inserted his shaft into her tight passage.

Chapter 45

The man couldn't help but let out a satisfied "Oh..." sound, apparently delighted by the tightness.

The doggy style position made it effortless for him, but he was very gentle in his movements, afraid of hurting the delicate back hole. He even paused for a moment, giving her time to adjust.

Once he sensed that she was not as tense anymore, he began to move slowly.

"Kitty, you were so loud just now. I heard Mrs. Black next door complaining... Oh... But I think you don't need to pay attention to her. After all, she complained for a few minutes and then slept with her man."

"It's really debauched, bringing the whole neighborhood into public debauchery. Do you want to know what they say when they're fucking? They're talking about our neighbor Kitty. You can't tell normally, but she makes such lewd noises when a man fucks her. I saw you with a man before and guessed it might be that muscular and capable man who's fucking you."

"Oh... which muscular and capable man is it? Has he fucked Kitty too? Did he fuck you so good? I'm curious..."

Kitty White clenched her lips tightly, finding it hard to bear hearing these obscene words coming out of the other person's mouth.

Not just her gradually loosening back hole, but also mentally, when she heard the other person say that the neighbors were also having sex, and even guessed about her own bedroom activities, she involuntarily tightened her hole, wrapping the shaft even tighter.

She felt an overwhelming excitement, as if falling from grace. Hearing those words from Perry's mouth was already a shock, let alone discovering that familiar people were secretly observing her and even mentioning her name while engaged in intimate acts.

Just thinking about all this, she felt like she was about to climax.

Trembling with a coquettish tone, she answered him, her voice filled with a playful meaning, "Yes, we had sex... but it was just a mistake. It's all because his cock was too big. I couldn't resist and agreed to him. If I had met you earlier, I would never have let him fuck me. Honey, trust me."

"Oh? How did he fuck you? When did you guys have sex?"

Kitty White didn't know what came over her. Even though there was a cock in her back hole, when Perry mentioned Tony Wilson, she felt a bit empty in her pussy. With one hand, she touched her muddy cunt, and after a few strokes on her tender pussy, she inserted her middle and ring fingers in.

She coordinated the movement, the wet sounds of her fingers matching Perry's rhythm. While fingering herself, she honestly described how the other man had fucked her.

"We don't fuck each other often. Usually, he comes to me. He's a man who is very faithful to his desires. His cock is like a donkey's dick, big and long. Every time it goes in, it feels unbearable, but once the glans is inside, it becomes smoother. Oh... Perry, you're too heavy... Oh... my God..."

As Kitty White was savoring the memory of Tony Wilson's cock, the man suddenly thrust into her forcefully. Actually, her back hole couldn't feel much pleasure, but there was something called a "brain orgasm." When she felt the friction of the cock against her colon, it instantly reminded her of the sensation of that big thing scurrying around in her pussy. Naturally, her heart melted, her legs weakened, and she wished the man would thrust a few more times.

Her fingers found her sensitive flesh, relentlessly teasing that area. While moaning, she continued to describe, "He always likes to pin me down and fuck me hard with his big cock. It lasts for a long time, every time making me feel like I'm going to be fucked to death. When I can't take it anymore, I tighten my juicy pussy, letting my juices flow as he ejaculates inside me. At that moment, he ruthlessly fucks my womb, shooting all his cum inside."

As she said that, Kitty White suddenly felt the cock of the man behind her move, as if he had been stimulated and started fucking her at lightning speed. Her lower body made a slapping sound as he pounded her. She knew he was about to cum, so she tightened her already tight back hole, just as she had described earlier. After about a dozen thrusts, a powerful liquid spurts out into her intestines, making her moan uncontrollably.

She still felt empty in her pussy. Even though she had been fucking herself for a while, it just wasn't enough for someone who was used to large cocks.

The man had pulled out his cock, still hard, and was rubbing it against the woman's pussy lips. She was happy about it and was about to move her butt backwards, wanting to take the cock inside her pussy, but the man backed away.

Kitty White was confused, but she stopped moving. The man then moved his cock back to tease her pussy lips, which was really teasing her.

Kitty White was about to cry out, wanting the big cock to immediately penetrate her pussy and fill her up, feeling the hot sensation of the cock tightly grasped inside her.

Unfortunately, the man was not going to satisfy her so easily. He still had a gentle tone, as if he was not the one who forcefully thrust his cock into her back hole earlier. He held his cock and rubbed it against her pussy, saying, "You say you enjoyed being fucked by another man's cock and claim that you love Priapus the most. You're such an unfaithful and lascivious girl. Prove it to me, show me your heart."

When Kitty White heard the word "Priapus," her mind instantly became much clearer. This was the first time her boyfriend, who suddenly appeared and looked exactly like Priapus, mentioned the original Priapus. She still maintained the position of her raised ass being rubbed by the cock, but she felt something was off the next moment.

Sure enough, when she turned around, there was no sign of the man anymore.

She was dumbfounded. If it weren't for the male products gradually acquired in her house over the past two days, she would have thought she had just had a long erotic dream.

She woke up in confusion and tidied herself up before taking a shower, trying to get rid of the dirty thoughts in her mind. Then she opened the floral curtain.

She saw the deity sitting on the stone platform, with a slightly opened red vertical scar on its chest, revealing a deep and unfathomable black crack in the middle.

Chapter 46

Kitty White felt a little panicky. She didn't know what had caused the change in the deity.

Thinking of Perry's sudden disappearance, she had to suspect that the answer was hidden in the last words Perry had left behind.

At this moment, she deeply regretted it. If she had known that one day she would seek the god, and the deity would favor her to such an extent, even observing her and fulfilling her desires, she would never have slept with other men.

It was such a loss just to make the deity angry!

She regretted it so much now, but there was no good way to remedy it. After all, how could she prove her heart?

It seemed like Perry and the deity could hear the voice deep inside human hearts. She had been devout, and Perry had even said that she loved Priapus the most!

With worry for the future and for Priapus, Kitty White had not had a peaceful few days.

Especially after receiving financial support from Perry, she had reduced the frequency of seeking work. However, she didn't want to sit empty-handed, especially when Perry suddenly disappeared.

So today, she decided to go to work. Although she hadn't been there for a few days, the foreman still recommended her for a good job as usual.

As a result, she felt that Priapus had not completely abandoned her and was still blessing her.

So her originally listless mood improved a lot, and she began to work with spirit and enthusiasm.

After a day of hard work, she came home to a cold room and suddenly felt a bit aggrieved. But she still devoutly lit incense for Priapus.

The vertical scar on its forehead seemed to have widened today, which worried her.

The following days were all the same, smooth but boring, until one day, on her way home, she was stopped by Tony Wilson again.

This man's intentions were very direct. She even noticed that his pants were already tented.

But she didn't give him a friendly face, just walked straight ahead. When he tried to grab her again, she looked at him with an unprecedented cold gaze and said, "Don't ever come find me again. I won't have sex with you. Go find someone else!"

Tony Wilson was frozen by her gaze, his face full of grievances and confusion. He didn't understand why she suddenly became so resolute. When he wanted to catch up with her, he remembered her icy eyes and stopped in his tracks.

Back home, Kitty White stood in front of the curtain, quietly standing for a while, as if she had made a decision. She paused for a moment, then headed towards the adjacent bathroom.

After taking a thorough shower, she adjusted her mood and confirmed that she truly missed Perry and reaffirmed her faith in Priapus. With her body naked, she lifted the floral curtain.

Chapter 47

"Believer Kitty White, I really don't know how to offer my sincerest faith, but I still want to say to the god that you are my ultimate belief. I am willing to entrust everything to you, including myself. I love you, I love Perry, and I want to prove it to you..."

Without grabbing the incense from the nearby shelf, Kitty White, after expressing her determination to the statue, did something unusual and daring. She extended her hand towards the statue that she had not touched since retrieving it.

Perhaps it was the power of the god, but the statue remained dust-free. In any case, it was the most exquisite statue she had ever seen, and of course, Priapus was the most handsome and kind god she had ever encountered.

Her slender fingers caressed the statue's eyebrows, eyes, and flowing hair one by one. Then she moved to its arms and chest. Her hands trembled, and she knew what her actions meant—

—This was blasphemous!

But since the moment she made up her mind, she had no intention of stepping back.

So after tenderly touching the statue with her fingers, she kissed it with her soft lips and devout love.

She even used her tongue to explore between the statue's legs, which were parted due to its seated position, licking the meticulously carved cock.

Then, with flushed cheeks, she positioned the statue between her legs, assuming a kneeling posture herself. Her soaking wet entrance constantly dripped onto the ground. When she aimed the statue at her own opening, it became tainted with human female fluids.

Kitty White was already immersed in her imagination of merging with Priapus. Even before penetration, she was already feeling pleasure.

She gripped the statue and slid its top back and forth between her swollen folds.

A large amount of fluids gushed out due to the pleasure and dripped onto the statue. Gradually, Kitty White even felt that she couldn't hold onto the statue properly. Sometimes her hand slipped, and the statue would press against her sensitive clit, giving her a genuine sense of being teased.

"Oh, Fuck me! Priapus, fuck me. I just want you to fuck me...Perry...Oh, my God..."

Moaning shamelessly, she tried her best to hold onto the base of the statue. Eventually, she thought it would be easier to operate if she placed it directly on the floor.

At that moment, she didn't care about anything else and didn't even consider the disrespect of placing the statue directly on the floor. She just held onto the statue and positioned it towards her entrance, then sat down.

"Oh... It's inside... Priapus is inside!! My god... it feels so good, filling me up... this believer's pussy wants to be fucked," she exclaimed.

While supporting the statue, she moved her hips up and down, making the statue enter and exit her pussy, leaving a trail of her arousal.

The statue was now completely unrecognizable. Hair, legs, chest – they were all covered in her juices. Some had become slightly sticky and frothy from the back and forth thrusting, hanging as foam on her shoulders.

Kitty White felt that this was the kind of solace she desired. It was the unparalleled solace that Perry had given her that day. She wanted to dedicate herself completely to it.

Just the statue alone could bring her such pleasure. Truly, it was her god. It was a pity that Perry wasn't there; otherwise, she could use the statue to please herself on Mondays, Wednesdays, and Fridays while riding Perry's big cock on Tuesdays, Thursdays, and Saturdays!

Or perhaps, they could pleasure themselves together – one penetrating her from the front while the other filled her from behind. It would undoubtedly be an unimaginably exquisite sensation.

She imagined it and quickly reached orgasm. In that instant, she lost control and completely sat on top of the statue. The top of the statue plunged deep inside her as the intense stimulation caused Kitty White to climax once again in a short period of time.

She sat there in a daze, her pussy filled only with the image of her god, yet she felt immensely satisfied in her heart.

Chapter 48

Tony Wilson was extremely shocked. He had followed Kitty White because he was worried about her abnormal behavior, but he never expected that she hadn't locked the door, allowing him to witness her blasphemous act towards the god.

As he listened to her vulgar words and watched her relentless twisting naked body, his gaze shifted to beneath her. He could vaguely see a stone flower platform, while the rest of it was completely engulfed by her slutty pussy, causing her to have an expression of utter ecstasy. Tony Wilson desperately wanted to rush forward and fuck her.

But he couldn't. He thought back to her gradually becoming more and more strange in her behavior, and he heard from the workers they employed together that they hadn't seen her for a while. Based on her diligent nature, it was impossible for her to abandon her work just because she had obtained a god's protection.

Furthermore, he wouldn't say that he knew Kitty White extremely well, but he did have a general understanding of her. Kitty White was somewhat selfish and self-seeking, just like him. They were both people who were loyal to their own desires and would fight for what they wanted. And if good things were handed to them on a platter, they wouldn't refuse.

He had always known that this woman was toying with him, but so what? They were so similar to each other, and he naturally understood her behavior of accepting gifts without agreeing to a relationship. He also enjoyed this feeling of being together without any official commitment. Every time he fucked her, he had a sense of taboo as if he were fucking someone else's future wife.

But now, this woman, with such a character, was resolutely trying to distance herself from him. He just couldn't understand her reason for doing so.

Until he saw Kitty White shoving the god statue into her own pussy.

No true devotee of a righteous god would desire the god like that. He was certain that the god she had brought back must be an evil god.

This raises a question – what should one do when they have invited an evil god?

Of course, the best option is to take it to a shrine for a sealing ceremony. However, for various reasons, not every evil god can be successfully sealed. With a mindset of wanting to give it a try, Tony Wilson went to the shrine the next day.

He arrived at the shrine early, and the staff inside were meticulously inserting incense into the censers. The scent of the incense gradually grew stronger, filling his nostrils with ashes, but he only furrowed his brow slightly.

After hearing Tony Wilson's request, the staff asked for the name of the god statue. When they heard it was Priapus, their expression became extremely strange.

The staff placed their hand inside their wide sleeve and looked at Tony Wilson with an expression he couldn't understand, saying, "Priapus is the most special god here. It's not one of our stored gods. It appeared in our shrine on a certain day on its own."

Seeing Tony Wilson's astonishment, they added, "But I don't think it's an evil god, because there have been women who requested him before. Although they were returned shortly after, the devotees who returned him showed great reverence towards him. They expressed gratitude to the god and regret and guilt for not being able to continue worshiping Priapus."

Tony Wilson found it very strange and asked in confusion, "Weren't they grateful to him? Why couldn't they continue worshiping? Was it because of financial reasons?"

The staff shook their head, indicating that they didn't know either, "In any case, many people have taken him away, but he has always been returned. He is the only god statue with a record of being returned."

Perhaps to reassure Tony Wilson, the staff recalled and continued, "In short, there have been no incidents of life-threatening events because of Priapus. Despite his strange appearance, he is indeed a highly esteemed god."

Chapter 49

After not getting the desired result at the shrine, Tony Wilson returned to the neighborhood where he rented a place, heavy-hearted. It should have been lunchtime, and he was starting to feel hungry. Instead of rushing to find Kitty White, he decided to satisfy his hunger first.

The street seemed unusually quiet today. He noticed that many of the small stalls that are usually open were closed.

Initially, he didn't pay much attention, as his mind was still occupied with thoughts of helping Kitty White with the evil god situation. But when he finally snapped out of it, he realized that the few people on the street had dwindled down to just him.

Standing at a crossroads, he saw a wide, well-trodden road to the left and a row of small stalls made of wood on the right. But regardless of which side he looked, he couldn't see a single person.

What should have been a lively lunchtime felt as if the whole world had disappeared, leaving only him.

Cold sweat started to trickle down his forehead, his heart racing. He quickly turned and started to walk back, reassuring himself with muttered words, "It's alright, just go home. Maybe it's some kind of holiday! Everyone must be busy! That's definitely it!"

Deep down, he knew something was wrong, but he still believed that as long as he went home and rested, things would be better tomorrow.

Everything was fine in the morning, so why had it turned like this?

When did things start going wrong... It was as if when he got off the car...

Tony Wilson, who was eager to quickly return home and escape this eerie situation, didn't notice that the route he was taking was gradually changing.

The familiar path to his home, in his eyes, started to distort, shedding its façade. The ground he stepped on, the surroundings he passed through, all became tinged with a layer of blood-red.

The blood-red pulsated faintly, as if the beating pulse of a human. He walked in a red, wet and sticky corridor, getting further and further away from his intended destination.

For the first time, he felt that the journey home was so long. His steps grew heavier and heavier. He didn't know how long he had been walking alone on this path, but finally, he saw his own door. He smiled with joy.

Kitty White was very happy. She felt that she had regained the meaning of life.

Since she had merged with the statue, she believed that she had an intimate relationship with Priapus. So she moved the shrine to her bed.

Now, every day, she could see Priapus when she fell asleep and woke up. Occasionally, Perry would appear and embrace her. She didn't need to work to get the food she wanted, nor did she need to struggle for warmth and sustenance. She could enjoy herself with the person she adored. This was her ideal life.

On this day, after finishing her lunch, she felt a slight boredom. The surroundings were so quiet, as if she was the only person living here.

But she knew it wasn't like that. It was her considerate deity who was worried that she would be disturbed by noisy sounds, so he had shielded her surroundings.

She was very grateful for this, but over time, she occasionally found this kind of silence a little frightening.

This is not right.

She reflected in her heart. Her deity had shown such consideration for her, so how could she still be unsatisfied? Didn't she used to complain that it was herself, not others, who made the surroundings so noisy!

With nothing to do, she found herself lying back on the bed. As she turned to her side, she looked at the statue on the pillow, and her gaze gradually softened.

At this moment, her heart was filled with love. But in the next second, the love was engulfed by a rushing desire. Her eyes turned an abnormal crimson, veins popping on her forehead. All her own thoughts in her brain drifted away, covered by layers of desire.

Unconsciously, she raised her finger and reached towards the cracked brow of the statue. She did not realize that the soft and smooth sensation she touched was not the hard touch of the statue, but belonged to human skin.

The man with shoulder-length brown hair, bare and sexy upper body, was sitting on an enlarged stone platform. The vertical scar on his forehead slightly opened, as if there was a suction force when the woman reached out. He supported his cheek and looked at the woman, whose arms were still speaking of her love for him, even after being swallowed. The blood-red pupils revealed no emotions. Until the woman disappeared, he felt a surge of satiation rising, and then he returned to the appearance of a statue.

The room fell back into silence, and all the illusions lost their effectiveness. The dusty room seemed like it hadn't been cleaned in a long time. There were rotting leaves in the dish on the table, and the insects crawling underneath made faint sounds.

"Priapus, the god of good luck and wealth, must be devoutly worshipped with three incense sticks and offerings at dawn and dusk every day. With its all-knowing and all-powerful, it is worshipped by those destined to..."

"What is this...?"

"This morning, a devotee named Kitty White returned it, saying that due to personal reasons, she couldn't continue to worship it. She praised this deity greatly and expressed regret for not being able to continue the worship. She hopes we can take care of it."

"What a strange person. If she cares so much, why did she return it?"

"Who knows... But this statue looks really frightening! Let's hurry and put it away..."

Story Six: Her In The Rain

Chapter 50

Water, clear, flowing, and soothing to the soul.

Verna Clark grew up in a remote village in a small town, living with her grandparents. Her parents, it was said, couldn't withstand the poverty and went to work outside the village, never to return.

In those days, with only two elderly people and a young child left in the house, they didn't report it to the police nor had the awareness to do so. They would just hold Verna Clark on their knees on rainy days and say, "It's raining again. The day your parents left, it was pouring so heavily that even the umbrella couldn't shield them, but they still had to go."

Verna Clark would listen to her grandmother repeatedly complain to her, "What's wrong with farming? Why can't farming sustain us anymore? Look at how well the old man and I have raised you!"

There seemed to be a hidden rivalry in her words, maybe with herself.

Anyway, Verna Clark didn't understand.

She was still young then, and her memories were filled with carefree happiness. During the holidays, she would run wild with her village friends, like a little boy.

To go to school, they had to walk several miles, setting off before dawn. Unlike in the city where someone would pick them up every day, the children in the countryside walked to school together and made plans to return together after school.

Verna Clark had a few good playmates, and they went to school and returned together. Sometimes, when it rained, they had to wear long rain boots made of a very firm material that didn't quite fit well, but they were cheap and affordable for every household.

The only downside was that they got muddy easily. Perhaps that was the only unpleasant thing about rainy days.

The rural roads were all dirt roads, and once it rained, they would become extremely muddy. It was slippery and easy to sink into the mud when stepping on it. The children would walk with one foot deep and one foot shallow. If they walked for a while, their rain boots would be covered in mud. If they didn't clean it off in time, it would weigh down their feet, making it difficult to lift them. Luckily, there were some puddles by the roadside.

Small puddles and some two or three-meter-deep pits that were dug to store manure. They couldn't really be called pits, just square or round deep holes that hadn't been used.

They always managed to find these kinds of holes. When they saw a big hole filled with rainwater, they would carefully place their feet, wearing rain boots, inside and swish them around twice. Thick mud would disperse into the water, and whatever remained would be stomped off on a hard surface nearby.

Everyone did this. It was definitely much more convenient than using a stick to forcefully scrape off the mud from their shoes.

Until one time, because it was too slippery due to the rain, she couldn't steady herself without holding onto anything, and her feet slid forward. She couldn't control it and fell into the deep pit filled with rainwater.

Her little companions were shocked, with no adults around. They stood there trembling, whether from cold or fright.

But Verna Clark, who had fallen into the water, was surprisingly calm. It was as if she didn't yet understand the meaning of death. When she was submerged in the water, what flashed through her mind was the television program about swimming, where they mentioned holding your breath underwater, or else you would drown.

She obediently held her breath and didn't dare to open her eyes. She floated and sank in the water, feeling only the coldness of the water, but strangely, not feeling afraid.

Then she was rescued.

Although there were few pedestrians on rainy days, there would still be one or two. They would see a group of children standing still, and a couple of them crying, so they would come over to take a look. They never expected to save a life in the process.

Chapter 51

After being rescued, Verna Clark suddenly seemed to have a feeling of fear, although she didn't know what she was afraid of. She was probably around eight years old at that time.

Crying all the way back home, soaking wet, her grandmother was terrified. She scolded Verna for not being careful and cursed at the other kids who were with her for not holding her back in time.

What did the other children do wrong? They were just kids themselves, and there was no reason for the anger.

Because of this incident, the other children were strictly forbidden by their parents to play with her. Who knows if the overprotective grandmother would scold them again one day? It was unfair.

So, after turning eight, Verna Clark felt somewhat lonely. But she didn't blame her grandmother, she knew that her grandmother was afraid of her leaving, just like her missing parents.

She just didn't expect her grandmother to be the first one to leave.

Many things were not as she had imagined. Instead, there were often unexpected events that shattered the tranquility of life.

She was raised by her grandfather. But later on, her grandfather passed away, leaving her all alone. She would still sit under the eaves and watch the rain on rainy days, but there was no longer the sound of nagging in her ears.

Verna Clark felt a bit cold and hugged herself tightly.

Martin Edwards came here to sketch. As a wandering artist, he had traveled to many remote but beautiful places. Coming here was an accident.

Because of heavy rain, the road to town was blocked by a mudslide, and the car was running out of gas. So he had to search nearby and luckily found a place to stay.

The villagers here were very simple and enthusiastic. He didn't think it was right to stay for free in someone else's house and inconvenience them for food the past couple of days. So he gave them a few hundred dollars, but they refused to take it no matter what. It was only when he said he wanted to ask them to buy something for him that they reluctantly accepted.

The houses in the village were not far apart, each with its own yard. In the early morning, mist coiled around the towering trees, and the fog-like water clouds intertwined, giving a particularly artistic feeling. He even wanted to stay a little longer.

However, unexpectedly, there was something else that caught his attention, and that was the girl living in the neighboring courtyard.

She looked about twenty, very young, but her face was pale. It was the kind of paleness that comes from never seeing the sunlight, growing up in dark corners. It made people feel uncomfortable yet fascinated at the same time. Unconsciously, he became interested in her.

Perhaps he was the only one who felt this way, as no one else seemed to pay much attention to her.

The girl was very beautiful, a natural beauty without much makeup. But he had never seen her smile, even if they brushed past each other, it was as if she couldn't see anyone else.

But the more this was the case, the more he couldn't help but pay attention to her. He felt that the scenery here might really be captivating him, and he actually wanted to stay here a little longer.

Verna Clark had no idea that someone was silently observing her. She just went about her daily routine.

It had been raining a lot lately, and the roof was leaking a bit. She wanted to find someone to fix it, but the road to town was blocked, which made her a bit annoyed.

Chapter 52

Even though she had an umbrella, she still inevitably got a little wet from the rain. When she returned, she took off her clothes and went to the bathroom to prepare for a shower. Although the house was a bit run-down, she still had the necessary amenities.

The bathroom was very narrow, just enough for two people. The water tank had already been heated, and there was a cold water pipe next to it to adjust the temperature.

The hot water washed away the stickiness and dampness from her body, making it difficult to see her face clearly in the rising mist.

The water flowed from her collarbone, over her exquisite and rounded breasts, trickling down from her raised rosy nipples, and licking over her lower abdomen in waves. Finally, it disappeared along her fair and slender legs.

Water, clear and transparent, warm.

Verna Clark's hand gradually caressed her raised breasts, mixing with the sound of water. She felt a bit aroused. It was as if she had just felt a pair of warm hands touching her all over her body, which was both comfortable and tingling. Her lips slightly parted as she let out a soft gasp, her chest rising and falling. She couldn't help but grip the showerhead tightly, slightly trembling as she placed it between her thighs.

A powerful jet of water sprayed onto her pussy, with heat and forceful droplets splashing onto them. She couldn't help but take a step back from the stimulation. Then, biting her lip and with a hint of shyness, she used her free hand to part her folds. It was already wet there, not just from the hot water but also from the desire gradually swelling within her body. The desires turned into lustful juices flowing slowly from her opening, gradually blending with the pleasurable hot water. Only when she touched it did she realize how slippery her entrance was.

Verna Clark was somewhat intoxicated. She touched her tight hole, soaked with lustful juices. Perhaps she was already mentally prepared. This time, she aimed the water jet at her entrance. The passionate flow instantly rushed into her depths, pounding against untouched inner walls. She wanted to stop and savor this pleasure, but the water continued to flow endlessly. Unable to bear it, she pressed the showerhead against herself, her legs unconsciously clamping together. Once the overwhelming pleasure subsided, she became unsatisfied again.

This time, she wanted to be completely filled with the water, ideally filling her hole to the brim. She opened her entrance with one hand, directing the water jet inside, while her other hand inserted fingers into her hole, searching for the right angle. She knew there was a sensitive spot inside her that, when stimulated by her fingers, would quickly release a lot of water, bringing her to the brink of ecstasy.

This spot was relatively shallow, and as long as she controlled the direction, she was certain she could hit it.

After several rounds of exploration, when the powerful water jet sprayed onto her sensitive flesh, she couldn't help but let out a scream. However, she managed to steady herself and let the water continue to strike her tender spot. In the end, reaching the pinnacle of pleasure, she cummed so hard that her eyes rolled back, gushing a large amount of liquid from her opening, merging with the water flowing from the showerhead.

Martin Edwards faintly heard a woman's scream. He stood up and looked out the window, but there was no movement. He suspected that he might have misheard and sat back down to continue his painting.

These past few days, he had been completing unfinished artwork. He had an idea in mind that while he was still here, he wanted to paint a portrait of the girl living in the adjacent courtyard. He wanted to meticulously capture her appearance, so he had been working diligently.

Chapter 53

Exhausted, Verna Clark quickly returned to her room and fell asleep. In a half-dream state, she felt as if someone was fondling her breasts. She opened her eyes and recognized the face – it looked somewhat familiar, like her ex-boyfriend.

"What are you doing?"

Verna Clark pushed his hand away. The man's handsome face was filled with guilt as he caressed Verna Clark's cheek. He said, "Verna, I'm sorry. I still love you. It's all a misunderstanding. I've always wanted our first time to be on our wedding night, and I've fucked anyone else. Trust me."

Saying that, afraid that Verna Clark wouldn't believe him, he even grabbed her hand and placed it in his pants. "Verna, check for yourself. It's clean."

Under the dim yellow light, the man removed his pants, allowing the woman, who was also without pants, to hold his cock and inspect it. In this debauched scene, Verna Clark didn't find anything wrong with it. In fact, she leaned in to check if the shaft was clean.

The flesh-colored shaft stood erect, its tip becoming moist under the woman's gaze. Red droplets of fluid gradually emerged from the head of the penis. Verna Clark wrinkled her brow and leaned closer, giving it a lick. It didn't taste like much, but she didn't dislike it either.

She naturally cupped the male member with her hands and began sucking, while gently massaging the testicles below, hoping to extract more sexual fluids.

Her saliva mixed with the man's glandular secretions, hanging from the shaft. Verna Clark ate with seriousness and devotion.

Her pale face flushed slightly.

After she had been sucking him for a while, the man couldn't resist pulling his cock out of her mouth and coaxed her, saying, "Verna, let me fuck you, okay? Look how wet your little pussy is, leaking so much water. I'll plug it up for you."

As he spoke, he had already pushed Verna Clark down onto the bed and eagerly thrust himself inside.

Verna Clark felt the man's movements and manipulations on her body, but her mind was filled with the words 'plug it up'... It felt suffocating... as if she was submerged in water, unable to breathe.

"No... don't plug it up... don't stop the water... Oh, no!"

Drip.

Drip.

Drip.

...

Oh... it was just a dream...

Of course, it had to be a dream.

Verna Clark chuckled self-deprecatingly, paying no mind to her soaked body, as she got up to find a basin.

The spot where she had noticed a leaking water drip had been caught with a bucket. Perhaps it was raining heavily outside again, as even the roof directly in front of her bed was leaking, drenching her entire body.

Carrying the basin, she walked under the eaves and watched the splashes of water on the ground, feeling somewhat absent-minded.

The sky had already turned dark, and only the sound of rain remained, filling the silence. The raindrops splashed high.

That year...

Hmm... yes, that year, when her parents left, it seemed like it was raining this heavily too, right?

And Grandma and Grandpa, and... the day when she caught the man in bed with someone else...

The rain is so heavy.

She set the basin down, and strangely, the image of the erotic dream she had just had on the bed flashed through her mind.

That tingling sensation on her chest, was it from the water?

She took off her clothes and stood naked in the rain. She lay on the wet clothes, spreading her legs apart, allowing the large raindrops to fall freely on her skin, on her pussy. She spread open her flushed pussy, letting the rainwater slide into it, and she felt an incredible pleasure.

Chapter 54

Martin Edwards thought he must have been mistaken as the dense raindrops obstructed his vision.

He seemed to have seen the girl next door standing naked in the yard, and then...

He swallowed his saliva, feeling like he might be going crazy.

But he stood there for a while, until he saw the woman using her lower part to catch the rainwater. He couldn't bear it anymore, this was not something a man could endure!

So he rushed out, this must be the craziest thing he had ever done in his life. He didn't know if he would regret it later, but at this moment, he wouldn't regret it.

Verna Clark saw the young painter, who lived next door. She had heard the villagers talking about him, but she didn't expect him to be awake at this time, and to appear before her in such an embarrassing moment.

Martin Edwards looked at the woman's naked body in front of him. She was writhing with anticipation before she noticed him. Her wet hair clung to her fair body, and the glimpse of her little pussy was as beautiful as he had imagined. He couldn't help but take a few deep breaths, squat down, and kiss her lips.

Is it permissible?

It must be permissible.

Verna Clark felt the man's agile tongue enter her mouth, carrying the smell of rainwater, exploring every corner of her wet mouth. She felt the man's tongue sweep away her saliva, and they exchanged bodily fluids, passionately kissing in the rain.

She felt that she had thought of something.

Therefore, when Martin Edwards touched her pussy, she did not resist, but even held onto him tightly.

Having been painting for years, his fingers had developed calluses. These fingers suddenly entered her tight and slippery pussy, bringing Verna Clark a stimulation more vivid than in her dreams.

Most importantly, both of them were already drenched by the rain. Just the thought of rainwater following the man's knuckles and being sent deep into her pussy made Verna Clark unable to contain her pleasure.

His body had the smell of ink, while the woman's body was filled with the strong scent of water.

With one hand in the woman's pussy, he buried his head in her breasts, indulging in licking and sucking them. Occasionally, he would use his tongue to flick her nipples, which were covered in saliva and rainwater. He firmly held onto her soft and plump breasts and paid no attention to the woman's moans as he licked and sucked vigorously.

He never knew he could be so wild, just as Verna Clark never knew being sucked by a man would feel this way.

And this pleasure reached its peak when the man buried his head between her legs, taking a bite on her folds. His powerful lips and tongue slapped and sucked her delicate petals, occasionally nibbling and pulling on her clit, and sometimes forcefully pushing his tongue into her tight opening. All of this made her feel intense pleasure.

"Oh... I can't take it anymore...... Don't come... Oh, My..."

His eyes turned red, "Let me fuck you, just once, it'll feel so good..."

Afraid that Verna Clark would reject him again, he took off his wet pants and carried her, then abruptly thrust his cock into her.

Never before had she experienced something so large entering her. She couldn't bear it; her small hole tightened uncontrollably. However, she couldn't resist the pleasure she had just experienced. Her hole had already become wet and slippery. How could this stop the man's attack?

On the contrary, due to the tightening of her inner walls, the friction became even more intense. Her waist became weak with his entry.

Before she could even struggle, his shaft, still wet from the rain, pounded into her front hole. Strangely, it always stroked against her sensitive spot until it reached the depths of her womb. She didn't feel any pain, only a sense of pleasure, as if she had returned to that evening's moment of self-pleasure.

Not only did the man's shaft, but also her favorite rainwater, completely fill her small hole. She felt an immense sense of satisfaction in her heart. She wanted more, more of the large shaft to whip her freely, more rainwater to fill her. She started responding actively.

Every time the man pulled out and thrust back in, she would lift her lower body to meet him willingly, wanting him to penetrate deeper. Seeing the woman he desired being driven crazy by him, Martin Edwards felt a sense of achievement.

Taking advantage of the night, the two of them joined together passionately in the rain. The sleeping people wouldn't hear the sounds of their bodies colliding or the moans of satisfaction when he filled her with his thick essence.

Everything was concealed by the rainy night.

When they parted ways, Martin Edwards felt both happy and fulfilled. Surprisingly, she thanked him with a smile.

He felt he had a chance, although he didn't know why she was thanking him. Could it be because she had some strange fetish, like an addiction to sex...needing someone to relieve her, or she would feel uncomfortable?

Well, he had to admit that he had a wild imagination. He speculated randomly for a while, thinking about having more contact with her in the future. Maybe he could even bring her home as his girlfriend.

Falling asleep with beautiful hopes, he never expected to be greeted the next day not by a smile from the woman, but by news of her death.

When he heard the news, his brain buzzed, and he felt unsteady.

"Poor thing, why did she have to choose such a desperate path and commit suicide by jumping into the river, feeling so repressed."

"Who knows, maybe she had some mental issues. I heard she drowned the day before yesterday, and they only recovered her body today. They said she had a smile on her face when she died. Well, ever since her grandparents passed away, she started going out, and I heard her boyfriend cheated on her when she came back."

"You even know about that?"

"I heard it from someone. Apparently, her son's friend works in the same company as her."

"That's just adding to her misfortunes. But she has always been gloomy since she was a child, so it's not entirely surprising..."

"Well, now that she's gone, at least try to accumulate some good karma!"

......

Martin Edwards looked stunned as he listened to the murmurs around him. Suddenly, he felt a suffocating sensation.

The water was clear, gentle, flowing, and pleasing.

Verna Clark slowly sank to the bottom, a slight smile on her lips.

When will... the rain stop...

When will the rain stop...

Rain, please stop soon.

—-The End—